Charlotte needed proof of his love

He kissed her deeply, but then broke away from her and sat up.

"Craig?" she asked, staring at him with wide questioning eyes.

He trembled convulsively and slowly turned to look down at her. "No," he said shortly, his voice thick and uneven. "Not like this, Charlie."

"What—what do you mean?"

"Come here." He pulled her onto his lap and kissed her shoulder. "I want to make love to you, Charlie. But I want it to be for the right reasons. Can you understand that? Not out of jealousy or anger, but because that's what we both want. And in our own time, not because you're putting me through some kind of test, okay?"

She nodded, her eyes still wide with sexual arousal—and she wondered when, if ever, it would be the right time....

SALLY WENTWORTH began her publishing career at a Fleet Street newspaper in London, where she thrived in the hectic atmosphere. After her marriage, she and her husband moved to rural Hertfordshire, where Sally had been raised. Although she worked for the publisher of a group of magazines, the day soon came when her own writing claimed her energy and time. Her romance novels are often set in fascinating foreign locales.

Books by Sally Wentworth

Don't miss any of our special offers. Write to us at the following address for information on our newest releases.

Harlequin Reader Service
901 Fuhrmann Blvd., P.O. Box 1397, Buffalo, NY 14240
Canadian address: P.O. Box 603,
Fort Erie, Ont. L2A 5X3

SALLY WENTWORTH

the devil's shadow

Harlequin Books

TORONTO • NEW YORK • LONDON
AMSTERDAM • PARIS • SYDNEY • HAMBURG
STOCKHOLM • ATHENS • TOKYO • MILAN

Harlequin Presents first edition November 1989
ISBN 0-373-11220-3

Original hardcover edition published in 1988
by Mills & Boon Limited

CHAPTER ONE

CHARLOTTE PAGE had read a great many books in which the heroine fell in love with the hero at first sight, and she was quite confident that it would one day happen to her. And it did. When she was only sixteen.

It happened during the summer holidays, when the sun seemed to shine endlessly down from unclouded blue skies on to the long rose-coloured days of her girlhood. Charlotte had been for an early morning ride over the neighbouring hills and came cantering back to the Abbey, hungry, windswept, and quite unprepared for the fate that awaited her. Stabling her horse, she ran across the little bridge into the old stone building by the back way. Her room was on the second floor of the main tower and was reached by a narrow stone circular stairwell. She took the stairs three at a time, whistling happily, and wondering what she would find in the cake tin in the kitchen to stave off her hunger until lunch time.

She washed her hands in the old-fashioned basin covered in blue flowers, and was about to run down to the kitchen when she heard a car drive into the courtyard below. Curious, Charlotte went over to the window and pushed it wide, leaning out so that she could see. It was a car she hadn't seen before—a low, two-seater sports car with the hood down, dark blue and quite old, but with the rich burnish that only hours of loving care could give. The car drew up beside the steps leading to the

5

main door and a man got out, unfolding his tall frame
in the low car and vaulting lightly out without bothering
to open the door. He stood looking around him in be-
mused surprise, as everyone did when they came to the
Abbey for the first time. He looked first in front of him,
then to his left and right, and it wasn't until he turned
around to look behind him that Charlotte saw him fully
and fell instantly in love.

He was in his mid-twenties, she judged, only about
eight years or so older than her, but already there was
a masculine assurance in his broad shoulders and the
confident lift of his head. There was, too, an air of contained strength in his muscular body and the sharp, clean
set of his jaw. He had a wide forehead, straight brows
and a thin, angular nose, adding up to a very mascu-
linely handsome face. Charlotte was too far away to see
the colour of his eyes, and anyway he was facing the sun
and squinting up into it as his gaze travelled around the
ancient walls. He reached her, and Charlotte's heart
jumped as he began to raise a hand to shield his eyes to
take a better look. She was sure that this dark stranger
would immediately fall in love with her too, and she could
already see them living in perfect bliss and harmony for
the rest of their lives.

She waited in eager expectancy for him to betray his
emotions with a cry of recognition, or at the very least
a gasp of wonder as love smote him as blindingly as it
had her. But before he could take a proper look at her
the main door opened and he swung round eagerly as
Verity ran down the steps to meet him.

'Darling!'

Putting her arms round his neck, Verity held her hips against his for a moment as she laughed up at him, her mouth curving provocatively. The stranger smiled back at her for a moment, letting her tease him, then firmly put his hands on her waist and drew her to him to kiss her. It wasn't a kiss of strangers, Charlotte was old enough to realise that, but she wasn't experienced enough to know whether it was the kiss of established lovers, or a promise that love was to come.

Pulling back from the window, she leant against the cool walls, her heart churning, her head dizzy. She ought to have known that any good-looking young man coming to the Abbey must have come to see Verity. But her sister hadn't mentioned that she'd invited anyone when she'd turned up the evening before, arriving without any warning as she always did, just before dinner, so that Renate, their German housekeeper, had had to rush around to prepare extra food for her. Verity hadn't cared, of course, and neither had their father, who was always too happy that his beautiful, spoiled elder daughter had bothered to come home to see him. But even he must realise by now that Verity only came home when she ran out of money or wanted to impress a new man—usually both.

Charlotte hadn't cared much before. Verity was Verity—too beautiful to be anything but spoiled by everyone who knew her. Sometimes Charlotte hero-worshipped her like everybody else, sometimes she hated her—like now. Her hands clenched, Charlotte ventured a quick look out of the window and saw that her sister was drawing the stranger into the house, her arm linked in his, her shining blonde hair caressing her shoulders as she tilted her head to look at him possessively. In that moment, as she saw the way her sister looked at this man *she* had fallen in love with, Charlotte's heart filled with a black hatred for her sister, an emotion far stronger than her usual jealousy.

Looking at herself in the full-length mirror, Charlotte stared in disgusted hopelessness at her tall, rather pudgy figure in the torn and stained jeans and school T-shirt. She was fat, downright fat, whereas their father was fond of saying that Verity had a figure like a willow. And Verity looked fabulous in a bikini. Whenever Charlotte ventured to wear one, she always felt terribly conscious of her boobs, which seemed to hang on her like grapefruit. And whenever she went out with boys they were always trying to touch them.

Her face, too, was plain compared to her sister's. Verity had perfect features, as their father, who was a writer was always telling everyone. She was his 'most beautiful creation', his 'child divinely fair'. His eyes lit up when Verity came into the room, but when he looked at Charlotte he would sigh and give a disappointed shake of his head. He never complained about her appearance, though, but then he didn't have to; Charlotte was fully aware that she was too plump, that her face was too tanned and full of freckles, and that her hair had too much red in it for her ever to be as silvery fair as Verity.

Anger ran through her as she looked at her reflection. She felt like throwing something at the mirror and shattering it. She wanted to be instantly remade into the sort of girl that the man in the car would take one look at and forget that Verity and her provocative smile ever existed. Running to the big old wardrobe, Charlotte yanked open the door and began to go frenziedly through her clothes, looking for something that would perform the miracle, but after only a couple of minutes she drew back and threw herself down on the bed in despair. It was no good. Nothing she could wear or do would make him even give her a second glance when her sister was around.

After a while despair gave way to anger; why did he have to come here when she was only sixteen? She just wasn't *ready* to fall in love. But then a new hope began to grow. If she had fallen in love at first sight, then surely he must too, even though he so obviously fancied her sister at the moment. It must have been *ordained* for him to come here so that she could fall in love with him. Therefore it must be so for him, too. Charlotte had been half inclined to stay in her room until he'd gone so that she didn't have the chagrin of watching him with Verity, but this new hope made her decide to go down to lunch, after all. And besides, she was growing extremely curious about the stranger. She wanted to find out his name, who he was, and to see the colour of his eyes.

Taking a dress from the wardrobe, Charlotte went to change into it, but then stopped; the dress was one of the few decent ones she had, but it was too old and too tight across the chest. And it was really too fussy for daytime, and Verity would know instantly that she had put it on to try and impress the stranger. Anyway, Charlotte tried to tell herself confidently as she went down the stone spiral staircase in only clean jeans and shirt, he would fall in love with her whatever she was wearing. The freckles and puppy fat wouldn't matter a bit, he would see straight through to her soul, and that would be *it*!

Reaching the door to the drawing-room, Charlotte hesitated a moment, then took a deep breath and walked in, expecting to see everyone already gathered there. But the stranger was alone. He was standing in front of the huge empty fireplace, a glass in his hand, trying to make out the worn escutcheon carved into the stone. He turned when he heard the door open, his face eager. Again Charlotte waited for some sign that he, too, had been brought here by fate to meet his heart's desire, but the eagerness faded out of his face and he merely nodded and said pleasantly, 'Hello there.'

The obvious disappointment that she wasn't Verity was the first really painful hurt that Charlotte's young heart had ever experienced. It hurt so much that she wanted to hurt back, and so she said in a harsh, disparaging voice that she couldn't control, 'Hello. I suppose you're Verity's latest.'

The dark brows drew into a frown. 'And you, I presume, are her precocious brat of a sister?'

Charlotte's face flamed and she would have turned to run, but the door opened behind her and her father and Verity came in. Verity was hanging on to her father's arm, much as she had hung on to the stranger's earlier, and she said eagerly, 'I've so been waiting for you two to meet. Daddy, this is Craig Bishop. And this is my very famous father, Hartford Page.'

'Oh, come now,' their father said in half-hearted modesty as he shook hands, 'you're exaggerating wildly again. You must take no notice of her, Craig. Verity always makes too much of those she loves.'

She doesn't make too much of me, Charlotte thought bitterly. But then, she's never shown that she loves me.

'I'm sure she doesn't exaggerate in the slightest,' Craig was saying smoothly. 'It's an honour to meet you, sir. Verity has told me a great deal about you, and I have, of course, read and enjoyed your books.'

Charlotte wondered what, if anything, Verity had said about *her*, and retreated behind a high-backed chair.

'How very kind of you to say so. And what do you do, Craig?'

'He's an architect, Daddy. And frightfully clever. You should see some of the wonderful buildings he's de-signed,' Verity said enthusiastically. 'Everyone says that he has a brilliant future.'

Craig smiled. 'And now I see what you mean about Verity, sir.'

Charlotte saw too, and wondered if Craig thought that Verity was in love with him. But he was far from being the first man her sister had brought home, and as far as Charlotte could see her behaviour towards Craig didn't seem to be much different than to the other men. She was always all over anything in trousers, Charlotte thought cynically, remembering a phrase she'd read somewhere. And they all seemed to love it, she realized, sinking back into sixteen-year-old pessimism.

'Oh, and this is my kid sister, Charlie,' Verity said offhandedly, as if she'd just remembered that Charlotte wasn't a piece of furniture.

'We met,' Craig acknowledged with a brief nod in her direction, then quickly turned to Verity again, a smile lighting his eyes.

Brown eyes, Charlotte saw. With curling dark lashes. And close to he was even more handsome than she'd first thought, his dark, luxuriantly curly hair a surprising contrast to his strong face. And yet it seemed right. Everything about him seemed right.

He was asking about the history of the house, and her father was immediately in his element as he explained that this was originally the Abbot's house in what had been a very large Abbey. 'I'm afraid the church itself and most of the buildings are just ruins now. We'll take you to see them after lunch, if you're interested. But I did manage to save this house from falling into ruin, too, when I bought it about twenty years ago.'

This was something of an exaggeration. Actually the house was in a perfectly presentable state when Hartford Page had seen and fallen in love with it a few years after his marriage. At the time he had been flush with the success of a new book and had mortgaged himself to the hilt to buy the house, without any thought to the costs involved in maintaining such a place as well as bringing up a family. The result had been a hand-to-mouth existence, with any money that came in having to be spent on repairing the roof or mending the walls. And the place was always cold. The walls were so thick and the windows so small that even in summer it didn't get warm. His wife had begged him time and again to sell it, but he wouldn't listen. He claimed that it gave him the inspiration to write. And maybe it did. He certainly spent most of his time in what had been the Abbot's parlour, a panelled room with a fire that was always lit and was the only warm and comfortable room in the house, a room where Hartford Page wasn't to be disturbed for anything until he emerged for lunch or dinner. But he loved showing people round the house and encouraged weekend visitors, another cross his wife had to bear, until she died from pneumonia, brought on by a cold followed by 'flu.

Charlotte had been ten at the time and had immediately been sent away to school, but Verity, who was six years older, had gone to a drama college, and was now quite a successful actress. She had learnt her craft so well, in fact, that Charlotte often found it difficult to tell whether or not her sister was acting a part. Sometimes she even thought that Verity didn't know herself. Like now.

As they sat down to lunch in the small dining-room overlooking the courtyard, Charlotte watched her sister as she kept the two men entertained, her father on her right, Craig on her left. She was very clever, Charlotte had to admit that, telling amusing anecdotes and dropping the occasional big name, so that both men hung on her words, laughing in all the right places and thoroughly enjoying themselves.

'I'm trying to persuade Craig to stay for a couple of days,' Verity said to her father. 'Help me to persuade him, Daddy. I don't have to be back in London until Tuesday, so it would be fun if we could drive back together on Monday evening.'

'By all means, my dear chap,' Hartford Page said expansively. 'You're most welcome.'

'That's very kind of you, sir. But I don't want to put you to any trouble.'

'No trouble at all. We always have a room prepared for guests.'

'Thank you. In that case I should very much like to stay—but only until Sunday evening, I'm afraid. I have an important meeting I have to go to on Monday.'

Verity pouted at him. 'Surely you can skip it? You'd have to if your car broke down or you were ill.'

Craig laughed at her. 'Don't tempt me!'

'Oh, but I certainly will if it means that you'll stay another day,' Verity returned, smiling into his eyes.

Their gazes held until Charlotte deliberately knocked over her glass of water.

'Oh, Charlie, you are clumsy!' Verity exclaimed. 'Use your napkin to mop it up.' Taking notice of her for the first time, she saw Charlotte's almost untouched plate. 'You've hardly eaten a thing. Don't you like it?'

'It's OK, I'm just not hungry.'

'Good grief! Are you feeling ill?' Without waiting for an answer, Verity turned to Craig. 'Usually she eats like a horse. But then she spends all her time when she's at home in the stables, so it's hardly surprising.'

'Are you keen on riding?' Craig asked, turning to Charlotte and showing a flicker of interest in his brown eyes.

'Yes. Are—are you?'

'Very much so. I go in for point-to-point racing whenever I can get a ride.'

'How super!' Verity broke in. 'We must go for a long ride tomorrow. I'm sure we'll be able to borrow a horse that will carry you from some friends who have a farm not far away.'

Charlotte gave her an indignant look; they only had the one horse which she looked on as her own, and if Verity took it the poor animal would be too tired for her to ride it afterwards. She opened her mouth to say so, but before she could do so, Verity cut in, 'And I do think you might have changed before you came to lunch, Charlie. You always smell of horse. You could at least make an effort when we have a guest, even if you don't ordinarily.'

Charlotte felt angry colour rising in her face, but could only glare mutely at her sister. Her eyes glanced towards Craig, but he was looking at Verity, a slight frown between his brows.

Their father changed the subject adroitly; he didn't like scenes, even such a petty one as that, which was why he never told anyone off, and he soon had them talking smoothly of other things. But he frowned at Charlotte, blaming her for it, because Verity, of course, could do no wrong.

After lunch the three of them went off together to show Craig the house and ruins while Charlotte escaped outside, running through the ruins, over a wooden fence and up through the flower-filled meadow to the top of the hill overlooking the Abbey. Here she threw herself down on to the grass and gazed moodily back at the house. It lay in a beautiful setting, surrounded by a moat that had once been part of a river and one of the Abbey's boundaries. There were fruit trees still in what had been the monks' orchard, and fish still lived in the ponds they had fished. But the walls that guarded it were now fallen and all that was left of the once proud church were the bases of a few columns and doorways, most of the stone having been taken away by the cartload when the Abbey was torn down in the reign of Henry VIII.

The house itself, and a few outbuildings, were all that stood intact, big and rambling, cold and impractical. But Charlotte loved it, perhaps even more fiercely than her father did, even though she wasn't blind to its faults as he was. She could remember no other home and yearned for it intensely when she was away at school, longing to get back. But she still had another two years of education before she could come home for keeps. No amount of begging would persuade her father to let her leave before she had taken her A-level exams.

After about half an hour she saw the three of them come out of the house, her father leading while Verity followed with Craig. Charlotte's body stiffened as she watched, consumed with jealousy. If only she could be more like Verity! She tried to remember what her sister had been like at sixteen, but she had been away at school and Verity at college, so they had seen little of each other, and the six-year gap made them a century apart.

Craig was being more than necessarily attentive, in Charlotte's opinion, giving Verity a hand whenever they crossed a stony patch, and putting a casual arm round her waist as he pointed something out in the overgrown ruins.

Charlotte watched them as they wandered around; it was a long tour even for her father, it was a good hour before they finished and Hartford Page went back into the house. Craig and Verity went towards the house but then went through the old cloisters and across the bridge, turning to walk up to the farm to see if they could borrow a horse for Craig for tomorrow, presumably. Charlotte watched until they were out of sight, then rolled over on to her back and gazed up at the sky. The easy tears of adolescence pricked her eyes. Craig was so wonderful, so handsome. The kind of man that you dreamt about. She was quite sure that she would never love anyone else, and yet she'd made that stupid remark when she'd met him and now he didn't even like her!

She cried for a little because it helped, but after a while remembered that he would be here until tomorrow night. Perhaps she might be able to make him change his mind about her. If he ever took his eyes off Verity long enough. And if her sister didn't make disparaging remarks about her again so that she just looked like a stupid schoolgirl.

For dinner that evening Charlotte made a really special effort, spending ages in the bath and washing her hair. But then Renate banged on the bathroom door and told her to come and help with the vegetables, which meant that she had to peel the onions because they always affected Renate's eyes. Charlotte did them, but then got cornered into straining the soup, so that she had to rush upstairs at the last minute to wash again and change into the dress that she'd almost worn at lunch time. There wasn't time to blow-dry her hair, or to put on her make-up properly, because she was still new at it and it took her quite a time to get it right. Eight o'clock came and she rushed down, not looking at all as she'd intended.

She needn't have worried about being late; the three of them were sitting down on the big settee, looking at her father's cutting-book, which he only showed to people he liked. Craig was being suitably admiring, and Verity kept leaning against him as she leant across to point at something in the book. Her father glanced up as Charlotte came in and gave her a look of surprised approval when he saw the way she was dressed, then turned back to the book. But Charlotte's day was made when Craig said, 'Excuse me a moment,' got up and came over to her.

'Hello, Charlie. Would you like me to get you a drink?'

'Why—why, thank you. I'd like a gin and tonic, please,' she said in surprised recklessness.

Behind them, Verity laughed. 'Give her a sherry, darling. Sweet and small.'

An angry look came into Charlotte's eyes, but Craig actually winked and poured her a gin—quite a stiff one too. Charlotte grinned and Craig smiled back at her. It was the happiest moment of her life!

This boost to her confidence, such a small gesture in itself, did wonders for Charlotte's morale. She became quite talkative over dinner as she asked Craig about his horse-racing experiences.

'I'm very much an amateur,' he told her. 'I started by riding a friend's horse after he broke a leg one season, and had some success. That led on to other people offering me a race, and I ride whenever I can. Practising is sometimes difficult, though, because being an architect has to come first, of course.'

'Where do you race?' Charlotte asked, thinking she might be able to go and watch him if it wasn't too far away.

But Verity took the conversation out of her hands by saying, 'Yes, do tell us. Then the next time you take part we can make up a party. It will be fun. I can bring some of the girls from the show. Who else can we have? Perhaps some of the men from your firm?'

She began making plans until the outing became a settled thing, with Charlotte definitely not included.

The next time she tried to talk to Craig, Verity gave her a frowning look. 'Do you really think you ought to let Charlie have another glass of wine, Daddy? She's getting quite loquacious.'

This repressive remark naturally shut Charlotte up for a while, but her heart was beating with such excitement at being near Craig that again she couldn't eat, so the wine, on top of the gin, went straight to her head.

'Of course, we live quite an isolated life here,' her father was telling Craig. 'I don't go into the neighbouring towns unless I can't avoid it—they're all beginning to look so alike now. Pulling down the old buildings to make way for shopping precincts. Such monstrosities! And I only go to London when I have to see my publisher, and then I stay at my club. I can't stand plastic and chrome hotels, and insipid meals that all taste the same—if they have any taste at all.' His eyes widened as an idea hit him. 'Tell you what, my boy, why don't you design a *real* hotel, in the old tradition? I can see it now—comfort instead of practicality.'

'Colonnades instead of concrete,' Verity echoed, catching on to his enthusiasm.

Craig grinned and joined in, the three of them striking sparks off each other as they kept coming up with new ideas for their dream hotel.

Charlotte sat back in her seat and watched them, the wine making her feel slightly detached. They were all three good to look at; even her father, who was nearly sixty and quite grey, had a look of debonair charm about him still, and in his youth he had been quite dashing, apparently. Her mother had certainly fallen for him, quite fatally, and had been a willing slave to his whims and autocratic fancies. And Craig and Verity, of course, came quite definitely under the category of 'beautiful people', the one so fair and the other dark. Perhaps theirs was the attraction of opposites. But they were certainly attracted, that was easy enough for anyone to see by the way their eyes held and their hands touched. Once, when their father got up to get another bottle of wine, Verity leaned towards Craig, her lips pouting to be kissed, the candlelight glistening on her bare shoulders above her black velvet gown. Craig smiled, a crooked grin of a smile that gave him a knowing look. He didn't kiss Verity, but he mouthed something that only she could hear and made her give him an arch look and swirl her blonde hair in a gesture that reminded Charlotte of a frisky young horse.

No, Charlotte thought, I'm the ugly duckling here. But then she remembered that the ugly duckling had changed into a most beautiful swan, and she smiled to herself, wondering if that was an omen for the future.

'You're obviously thinking of something very pleasant.'

Craig's voice broke into her thoughts and she lifted her head to see him looking at her with a slightly indulgent smile.

'Yes, I am,' she acknowledged. 'I'm thinking about what it will be like when I'm as old as Verity.' She lowered her voice, not wanting her sister to hear, but Verity had turned to speak to Renate, who had come in to clear the plates.

'Do you want to be an actress, too? Or a writer?'

Charlotte shook her head decisively. 'No, I want a *steady* occupation where you know exactly how much money you're going to get instead of being rich one minute and poor the next.'

Craig laughed—he actually laughed at something *she'd* said. 'Perhaps you'd better be an accountant, then. Or better still, a computer programmer.'

'How dull!' Verity broke in, overhearing. 'That wouldn't suit me at all. Still, I suppose it might be all right for Charlie. If she ever stops being a tomboy.'

'I'm not a tomboy!'

Verity gave an amazed look. 'Good grief, Charlie, calling you a tomboy is being polite! I've never known anyone as hoydenish as you for your age. All you live for is horses. And you're so scatterbrained and clumsy that sometimes I think you'll never grow up! I'm even beginning...'

Charlotte stood up, her face white. 'I don't want any pudding. May I go, please?' she said, addressing her father, her napkin gripped tightly in her hands.

He nodded, sensing that she would go anyway, and quite glad to be rid of her when she seemed to upset Verity so much.

Running out of the room, Charlotte headed straight for the paddock, kicking off her shoes when she got to the grass so that she could run more easily. Her horse, Limbo, was grazing peacefully, and gave only a soft whinny of recognition as she put her arms around his thick neck. She buried her head against him, her nostrils filling with his warm, safe, familiar smell. It had always been the same, Charlotte thought wretchedly. Verity had been running her down and picking on her ever since she could remember. There had never been any sisterly love or even warmth between the two. And her father always sided with Verity, even though he did it in silence. Ever since her mother had died she had felt that she was on her own—no, less than that, she'd felt as if she was only tolerated, an unwelcome outsider who had to be suffered and provided for. Because she was so quiet and awkward, she supposed. Not lively and intelligent, and always full of new ideas, however fanciful, like Verity. And because she was so plain, not beautiful like Verity.

The horse stopped grazing and lifted its head, its ears pricked. Turning, Charlotte saw Craig climb the fence and walk across the paddock towards them in the last falling light of the long summer day. He flicked a glance at her to see if she was crying, and then gave all his attention to the horse. 'He's a fine fellow. What do you call him?'

'Limbo. Because when we first had him he seemed to be all limbs.'

'Who looks after him when you're away at school?'

'I have to loan him to a riding school. So when I'm on holiday he gets a holiday too.'

Craig raised his hands to hold the horse and stroke him gently, murmuring soothing words as he did so. A tremor of pleasure ran through the animal as he blew softly through his nostrils.

'He likes you!' Charlotte exclaimed.

'He knows I've got something for him.' And Craig took a carrot from his pocket and gave it to Limbo.

'You didn't bring that with you, did you?'

'No, your housekeeper—Renate, isn't it?—let me have it.'

'So you charmed her too,' Charlotte said without thinking.

He laughed. 'That's right. I'm a devil with horses and housekeepers.'

'And girls—women.'

Craig gave her an amused glance. 'Don't you believe it!'

'But you've charmed Verity.' Charlotte's hands tightened in the horse's mane. 'Are you in love with her?' she blurted out.

She gazed at him in the gathering dusk, her heart and breathing suspended as she waited for him to answer, but he only said, 'What's the matter between you two? Why does Verity give you such a hard time?'

Charlotte looked away and shrugged. 'I don't know. They expect me to be like them, I suppose. But I'm— I'm just not.'

There was a note of despair in her voice, and the 'they' had given a lot away. Putting a finger under her chin, Craig tilted up her face until she was looking at him. 'You're fine as you are. Maybe you're just a late developer. I'm certain that one day you'll be as beautiful as your sister and as clever as your father.'

'Do you really think so?' Charlotte asked with almost pathetic eagerness. But then she gave a small chuckle. 'It had better hurry up, I'm getting pretty old already!'

Craig laughed. 'It'll happen, believe me. But don't rush it—you've got plenty of time. Make the most of here and now.'

Charlotte fervently wished that here and now could go on for ever, standing in the twilight like this with Craig. As lightly as she could she said, 'And next I suppose you'll tell me that one day I'll meet a nice boy that I'll fall in love with and I'll live happily ever after?'

There was real amusement in Craig's voice as he said, 'Ah, I see you've heard it all before. So I'm wasting my time, am I?'

'No.' She shook her head, and in a sudden burst of longing, said, 'In fact, if I fall in love, I—I think I'd like it to be someone like you.'

Immediately appalled at what she'd dared to do, Charlotte waited in dread for him to laugh, but was infinitely grateful when he didn't, instead saying sincerely, 'Thank you. I'm very flattered. But like I said, Charlie...'

'Charlotte.'

'Sorry, Charlotte. As I said, you've got all the time in the world before you fall in love.'

There was almost a touch of sadness in Charlotte's voice as she shook her head and said firmly, 'No. It's already happened to me.'

'It has?' He turned to her in surprise, but she could hardly see his features, it was becoming so dark. 'But you said when you fall you...' He stopped, his eyes fixed on her face. 'Are you saying what I think you're saying?'

'Yes.' She gulped. 'I'm—I'm in love with you.'

'My dear girl!' Craig gazed at her in perplexity. 'But you can't...'

'I can. I have,' she broke in urgently. 'I'm sorry, but I can't help it.'

'Ah, no, don't say you're sorry. Never be sorry that you love someone.' He gave a rueful little smile and lifted his hand to gently push a loose tendril of hair off her face. 'Now I'm doubly flattered, but I think this is only a passing fancy. In time you'll meet lots of other boys that you'll like and...'

'No!' Charlotte almost stamped her foot in vexation. 'I don't want anyone else. I know I'm too young and everything and you don't like me much, but it ...'

'I *do* like you.' Putting his hands on either side of her head, Craig gazed down into her troubled, earnest young face. Then he gave a sort of laugh that was half a sigh and said, 'Here, this is to remember me by.' And he bent to place his lips against her and gently kiss her.

Charlotte immediately put her arms around his neck, moved close against him and kissed him back fiercely.

'Hey!' He broke loose from her hold, pulling her arms from around his neck and staring down at her. 'Hey!' he said again in a stunned kind of voice.

'Craig! Craig, where are you?'

Verity's voice called out to him from the bridge over the moat and he swung towards the sound, then looked back at Charlotte worriedly.

'You'd better go,' she said flatly. 'All Verity's men go running as soon as she calls them.'

Craig had been about to turn away, but he stopped and looked at her. '*All* her men?'

There was something in his voice that warned Charlotte not to go any further, to gloss over what she'd implied with a joke, but she was at an age when at one moment she was told to grow up and stop being childish, and the next that she was still only a schoolgirl. She felt that no one understood her, and resented the lack of understanding, not realising that she sometimes acted like a child still and sometimes like an adult, but mostly at the wrong times. And most of her resentment was centred on her sister. Whenever Verity came home she seemed to go out of her way to belittle Charlotte and show up her gaucheness, as if underlining her own elegance and beauty. And where Charlotte seemed to be hemmed in by school rules during term time and having to be in at certain times in the holidays, as well as having set chores to do in the house and garden, Verity had none of these things. She lived in London and came and went as she pleased, often going to all-night parties even when she was at the Abbey. No one told her off, she never had to give up anything she wanted to do to help Renate, and she always had loads of beautiful clothes and gorgeous boyfriends like Craig. And Charlotte didn't want her to have Craig, she desperately didn't want that.

So she looked at him and gave an incredulous laugh. 'Surely you know that Verity gets through men like...' But then she clapped a hand over her mouth as if in consternation. 'Oh, dear, perhaps I shouldn't have said that. Maybe you're gone on her *too*.'

The emphasis on the last word was faint but definite. Craig gave her an appraising look and Charlotte suddenly felt sick inside, but it was too late to turn back now even if she'd wanted to, because Craig said slowly, 'Does Verity have many—boyfriends?'

Charlotte laughed again, the high-pitched nervous giggle of a teenager. 'Well, I'd hardly call them *boys*. She usually goes for older men, businessmen and—and film producers, that kind of thing,' she told him, improvising hastily. 'You're really quite young for Verity.'

'And does she bring these men here?'

She was about to say yes, but saw him watching her warily, still half suspicious. So instead she said airily, 'Oh, no, not all of them. Only those she wants to impress. But she goes with men she knows round here too, of course. And that makes Tony really mad.'

'Tony?'

'Yes, he's the man who runs the farm up the road. You probably met him today when you went to borrow a horse. He's crazy about Verity—has been for years. Isn't it romantic?' Charlotte paused, knowing that she was on safe ground because it was quite true about Tony.

Craig was frowning thoughtfully, so maybe he had noticed that Tony was jealous. Laying it on thicker, Charlotte said, 'Tony wants Verity to marry him, but she won't, of course, because he wants her to give up acting. She'll never do that. But she still goes out with him when she has no one else. She stays out all night with him too, which isn't fair,' she added in genuine petulance. 'I always have to be in by ten-thirty—even at the weekends.'

'Craig!' Verity must have gone back into the house to look for him, but now she came out again, her voice coming nearer as she walked towards the paddock.

'I think I'll go for a ride,' Charlotte said nervously, and collected her shoes, then ran over to the stables to fetch her saddle and bridle.

Having tacked up the horse, she climbed easily on to its back. Craig opened the gate for her and she called goodnight as she trotted past, then dug her heels in and twitched on the reins to turn aside and avoid Verity.

When she came back an hour or so later, only the light above the porch was on. Charlotte let herself in quietly and crept up the stairs to her room. A light shone under the door and she thought she must have left it on earlier, but when she went in Verity was there—sitting in a chair waiting for her.

As Charlotte walked in, Verity got to her feet and gave the younger girl a stinging slap across the face, delivered with all the force of her arm.

'You little bitch!' she shouted furiously, and hit her again. 'I could kill you! How dare you go telling tales to Craig? Thanks to you we've had the hell of a row and he's gone back to London!' She tried to hit Charlotte again, but the other girl put up her arms to protect herself.

'I'm glad!' Charlotte yelled back. 'He's too nice to go out with you!'

'What the hell do you know about it? We were really getting somewhere until you put your nasty little spoke in.' Verity tried to kick Charlotte, who jumped quickly out of the way. 'You wait!' Verity threatened, her voice still trembling with fury. 'I'm going to get even with you for this, however long it takes!' And then she strode from the room, sending the door crashing to behind her.

Charlotte ran to lock it and then gave a great shout of joy. She whirled round the room in an ecstatic dance until she fell on the bed, giddy and panting for breath. It had worked! Even if she couldn't have Craig, neither could Verity now, and to her adolescent mind that was the most wonderful thing in the world.

CHAPTER TWO

IT WAS nearly six years before Charlotte met Craig again. He and Verity had never got back together, and anyway, it was only about six months afterwards that Verity had got a film part in America and had liked the country so much that she had decided to stay. She was quite successful now, according to the letters she wrote to their father, letters full of big names with whom she was on friendly terms, and with lots of titbits of gossip that he loved to repeat. She didn't write to Charlotte, though, and Charlotte didn't expect her to.

So much had happened to Charlotte in those years. She had got good grades at school, but instead of going to university had gone to a local technical college to take courses in computer studies and business management. From there she had got a good job in the financial department of a large company in a town only about half an hour from home. This enabled her to go on living at the Abbey, to ride in the summer evenings and at weekends, and to keep their father company, as well as helping with the upkeep of the house now that he wasn't writing so much.

He seemed to have lost a lot of his zest for living since Verity had gone away. Even his love for the Abbey seemed to have waned, and he often grew morose and short-tempered. Charlotte tried to stimulate him, but mostly got ignored; he would murmur that he had a book he wanted to read, and go off and leave her alone. It hurt at first that he wouldn't let her take Verity's place, but he gradually began to rely on her in many other ways, so that she felt happier than she had for years.

Charlotte had made lots of friends too, both at college and at work, and had several romances during those six years, but none of them had grown into anything very serious. But it was through an ex-boyfriend, Mike Brooks, that Charlotte met Craig again. Her horse, Limbo, had got too old to ride and Mike had put her in touch with a couple he knew who had a horse, but the wife was pregnant so couldn't exercise it. Charlotte had taken over the horse for a year and in the process had become friendly with its owners, Tina and Kevin Slater. They were very horsey people, often going to race meetings, gymkhanas, and horse shows, and Charlotte sometimes went with them, making up a four with Mike, with whom she was still friendly.

One sunny April day they decided to go to a race meeting at Sandown Park, and when Charlotte looked down the list of runners, there was Craig's name, down to ride. She gave an involuntary exclamation of surprise, making Tina ask her what was the matter.

'Oh, it's nothing. Just that I've met one of the riders.'

'Really. Who? Do I know him?'

'I shouldn't think so.' Reluctantly Charlotte pointed out his name.

'Craig Bishop. No, I haven't met him, but I've heard of him, of course. He's very good. And so is that horse he's riding, Blanico.' She turned to call to her husband. 'Kevin, Charlotte knows Craig Bishop. We must have a bet on him.'

It had been a long time since she'd seen him. The emotions that had surged through her when she'd fallen for Craig had gradually dwindled away. Other things, other people, had filled her life, and instead of thinking of him every day it had become once a week, then once a month, until she hardly thought of him at all; but she hadn't forgotten him. Odd things would bring him suddenly to mind, his features as vividly clear as the day she'd met him.

When the time for his race drew near she and Tina went down to watch the horses parade before the start, while the men went to place their bets. Some of the riders were already mounted, their shirts and caps bright with their owners' colours. Charlotte looked at their faces but didn't recognise Craig. Could he have changed so much that she didn't know him? Or had her memory played her tricks and turned him into something he wasn't?

But then Tina said, 'There he is—over there, talking to the woman in the fur coat. It looks like mink, too.'

Charlotte looked to where she pointed and saw a man in a shirt of pale and dark blue bands and a pale blue hat. He had his back to her as he talked to the woman, but then he nodded and turned to mount the horse so that Charlotte could see him properly. No, he hadn't changed. She would have known him anywhere, even though the dark curls were hidden by his cap. He heeled his horse, a big grey, into the circle of horses parading round, and glanced their way as he passed, but there was no recognition in his eyes.

'He didn't seem to remember you,' Tina said disappointedly. She loved getting to know other horsey people.

'I didn't expect him to,' Charlotte said with a laugh. 'I really don't know him at all well. He was a boyfriend of Verity's.'

'Oh, I see. But she's been in America for years, hasn't she? No wonder he didn't know you.'

No, it was hardly any wonder, Charlotte realised, because in six years, while Craig had hardly changed at all, she had changed a great deal. Not into a swan, but something far more exotic. Her puppy fat and awkwardness had long since gone, leaving her tall and graceful with a mane of red-gold hair. She wasn't soft and fragile like Verity, or even beautiful, but there was an arresting quality about her that made people look twice, and with men that second glance often lingered appreciatively. And she definitely wasn't a clinging vine type; there was an air of independence about her that women envied and men admired—until they realised she didn't need them.

They rejoined the men and watched the race from the stands, and although Charlotte was over him her hands still balled into tight fists of tension as she watched Craig race, only relaxing when he came safely, and first, past the winning post.

'He did it!' Tina exclaimed excitedly. 'We won!'

Delightedly they collected their winnings, and after the next race decided to celebrate with a bottle of champagne in the bar. They chose a table overlooking the course and began a friendly wrangle over which horses to back for the rest of the day's races. Other racegoers had decided to do the same thing and the room became quite crowded. The Slaters knew quite a few people there, some of whom joined their party and were introduced to Charlotte. One of these was an amateur jockey, and he was talking to Charlotte and some others sitting nearby when someone broke off to look round, and Charlotte lifted her head to find herself only a yard away from Craig.

His eyes went casually over the group of them and lingered for a moment on Charlotte, with interest but no flicker of recognition. He exchanged a few words with the jockey and then, evidently in no hurry, hooked up a chair and joined them. Several people congratulated him on his win and then the conversation became general again. Charlotte wasn't sitting near enough to him to talk to him personally. She was aware, though, that his eyes were often on her, but she deliberately avoided meeting his glance.

Just before the next race began the group broke up a little, some going down to the course to watch and others to place their bets. Tina, who was very pregnant, decided to stay where she was, so Charlotte had little choice but to stay with her when her husband went cheerfully off with some other men. Charlotte's escort, Mike Brooks, got them another drink, but when the race started he went outside to watch, while Tina got into a deep conversation about babies with the woman sitting on her other side. Craig, instead of leaving with the other jockey, moved to the seat next to Charlotte.

Her heart did a crazy kind of flutter and it took a lot of courage to meet his eyes when he said easily, 'I don't think we got around to being introduced properly. It's always the same in a crowd like this; somebody reels off a whole list of names and the only one you don't get is that of the person you really want to meet.' He smiled, confident in his masculinity, sure from past experience of his own attractiveness. "Mine's Craig Bishop,' he offered.

'Yes, I know.' Charlotte looked full into his face, but he still didn't remember her. 'I watched your race.'

'Did you have a bet on Blanico?'

'Yes, but nothing bank-breaking.'

He laughed. 'Well, I'm glad he won for you.' His eyes went over her with increased interest. 'Do you come for the social side or the horses?'

'Oh, the horses every time. They're always so full of health and are so beautifully turned out. And they enjoy themselves so much.' She spoke enthusiastically, her grey eyes lighting, but then remembered who she was with and flushed a little. 'But you know all that already.'

'Yes, but it's a refreshing change to find someone else who cares about the horses more than the racing. I don't think I've seen you at Sandown before, have I? I'm sure I would have remembered you if I had.'

Charlotte gave a small smile. 'No, you haven't seen me at Sandown before.'

There must have been an inflection in her voice that Craig picked up at once. 'But we've met somewhere else?' He frowned in an effort to recall it, but then shook his head. 'No, I'm sure we haven't. What *is* your name, by the way?'

She hesitated, wondering if even her name would mean anything to him now. Not hers, perhaps, but it would make him remember Verity. But with what emotions— sorrow, hate, or just simple nostalgia? Was Verity a love lost, or a love gratefully over? She was about to tell him when a burst of cheering heralded the end of the race and Mike came back into the bar to join her. He saw Craig and, although he and Charlotte were no more than friends now, decided to make it plain that he was with her.

'Marvellous race, Charlotte. You should have come and watched. The horse you fancied came in third.' He stood by Charlotte's chair in a proprietorial manner, but Craig made no effort to give him back his seat; in the end Mike had to go and sit on the other side of the table, where he began to talk to someone else.

'Charlotte?' Craig said in a low voice so that no one else could hear them. 'No, it doesn't ring a bell.' He glanced down at her ringless left hand and then gave a slight nod in Mike's direction. 'Boyfriend?'

'Ex.'

'Ah!' There was a wealth of meaning in that one syllable. 'But he's still possessive?'

Charlotte wondered in what sense he meant possessive, but she merely raised an eyebrow slightly and said, 'He brought me here.'

Craig glanced at Mike for a moment, but he was having an animated conversation with Kevin Slater and a couple of other men, his jealousy temporarily forgotten. Leaning forward, Craig gave her an almost challenging look. 'How would you like to come and meet Blanico?'

'He's still at the racecourse?'

'Yes. His trainer has another horse in the last race, so Blanico has to wait until then.'

'Are members of the public allowed down in the stalls? Surely the security people...'

'It will be OK as long as you're with me. Will you come?'

Again there was challenge in his voice and his dark eyes. She tried to decide, realising that this was the first move in a very original line. And if she agreed it might lead to—anything? Nothing? Probably the latter, when he found out who she was. But he was obviously determined to pursue it that far at least, and Charlotte decided that she would much rather be found out somewhere more private than this crowded racecourse bar. So she nodded. 'Yes, I'd like to.'

Craig grinned, and almost before Mike had realised what was happening he'd stood up and moved his chair out of the way, giving Charlotte room to get up and leave the bar with him.

'Charlotte!' She just caught Mike calling her name but decided to ignore it, allowing Craig to take her elbow and lead her through the maze of stands and boxes down past the jockeys' weighing and changing rooms and out to the stables where horses were waiting either to race or to go home. He spoke to one or two officials on the way, who gave Charlotte a look of amusement and let them pass.

Blanico was standing patiently in his stall, a blanket over his back, with an air of calm pride, as if he knew that he was big and beautiful and had done wonderfully well. Just like Craig, in fact, a thought that made Charlotte give a low chuckle as she went forward to stroke him. 'Hello, old fellow. Aren't you gorgeous?' The grey tossed his head as if in agreement and then nuzzled her jacket. 'No, I'm sorry, I don't have anything for you.' She turned to Craig. 'Haven't you got a carrot? You always used to carry them.'

He gave her a sharp glance, but produced a piece of carrot from the pocket of his jacket. Charlotte gave it to the horse, fussed him, and asked several questions about him which Craig answered evenly enough. But she was aware that he was waiting now and wasn't going to be put off from learning her identity any longer.

Finding nothing more to ask about the horse, she continued to stroke his nose, but turned to look at Craig. He was watching her quizzically as he leant against the wall, arms folded, ankles crossed as he waited. 'You don't really know me,' Charlotte told him. 'But you know—knew my sister. Verity Page.'

His eyes widened and he straightened up, his arms going down to his sides. 'Why, yes, but I . . .' But then his brow cleared as remembrance came. 'Of course— Charlie!' Other things came back to him, too. 'Ah, yes, I remember,' he said softly. His eyes lingered on her face as he began to smile. 'Oh, Charlie, how you've changed!'

'Just grown up, that's all,' she answered tightly.

'Grown beautiful,' he corrected. Leaning forward, he took hold of her hand and drew her towards him. 'Yes, it's all coming back to me. I can remember that night at the Abbey very well.'

Because that was the night he had broken up with Verity, Charlotte realised with a flash of jealousy that hurt even now. But at least he hadn't asked about Verity first; he had spoken only of herself. And it seemed that she was still on his mind, because he said, 'I suppose I ought not to remind you of it. Or even dare to hope that you might feel the same way.'

He was teasing her, she realised, but she wasn't to be drawn. 'A gentleman,' she said coolly, 'certainly wouldn't remind me of it.'

Craig laughed delightedly. 'Now I really am stuck! I can't win either way, can I?' His brown eyes travelled over her tall, slim figure appreciatively. 'I have to admit I didn't recognise you.'

'It was a long time ago.' She took her hand from his. 'And we only met briefly—for a few hours.'

'But it seemed that they were enough—for you.'

'I was very young and impressionable,' Charlotte answered lightly. 'Someone as—glamorous as you had never come my way before.'

Craig raised his eyebrows. 'I've never thought of myself as particularly glamorous.'

'Oh, only to young girls. And of course you're a great deal older now, too.'

'Ouch!' He grinned at her, not at all put out. 'You *have* grown up! You know, we have a lot to catch up on. How about having dinner with me so that we can start getting to know one another again?'

'Perhaps.' Charlotte gave the horse a last stroke and turned to walk back towards the stands.

'Only perhaps?' Craig asked, falling into step beside her. 'I could introduce you to lots more horses,' he tempted.

Charlotte laughed. 'That's certainly almost impossible to resist. But...' she shook her head, 'I don't know.'

'Why not?' Putting out an arm, Craig stopped her and turned her to face him. 'I promise not to take advantage of our previous meeting.'

'You already are.' She looked at him and realised that she had to tilt her head. 'You're awfully tall for a jockey.'

'Yes,' he acknowledged. 'Which is why I could never become a pro. But jump jockeys are allowed to be taller.' His eyes held hers. 'Stop evading the issue. When will you have dinner with me? Today? Tomorrow?'

Charlotte lowered her eyes, her heart thumping, realising that he still had the power to set her insides on fire. 'I haven't said that I will,' she prevaricated.

Craig gave her a keen look. 'Because of Verity?'

So the name was out in the open at last. Trying to shut the past out of her mind, Charlotte said slowly, 'Yes, I suppose so.'

Craig looked amused. 'I never saw her again after that night—except on the cinema screen. But I heard she went to work in the States. She's still there, isn't she?' Charlotte nodded and he lifted his other arm so that he had a hand on each of her shoulders. 'So why worry?' he said softly. 'Forget Verity. I want to get to know you, Charlie—very much.'

So he'd forgotten that she didn't like to be called Charlie. But it didn't matter. Looking up into his face and feeling his hands on her, Charlotte was filled with the tumultuous excitement that had lain dormant for so many years. Her heart swelled and her throat felt tight as she managed to say, 'All right. I'll—I'll have dinner with you.'

'Marvellous! When?' Craig slipped an arm lightly around her waist as they walked on. 'Tonight?'

'No, not tonight,' she laughed. 'I'm with Mike and a couple of friends. We've been invited back to their place for dinner. But I can make Saturday, if that's OK?'

'Of course.' His hand tightened a little. 'Just how ex is this Mike?'

Charlotte gave him a quick, rather surprised glance. He couldn't be jealous, so was he just being gallant—or making sure that he had a clear field? 'We were never that—close,' she said rather awkwardly. 'Now he's just a friend.'

'Good.' Craig's brown eyes smiled into hers. 'Because I'm beginning to be very glad that I've met you again, Charlie. I seem to remember telling you you'd grow into a beauty.'

'Hardly,' Charlotte protested. 'I'm no swan.'

'No.' He looked her over. 'You're far more exciting than a swan. More of a firebird, with that gorgeous flame of hair.'

'A firebird?' she questioned, using flippancy to hide her surging emotions. 'Don't they burn people?'

Smiling, he leant forward and just touched her lips with his, then said against her mouth, 'I'm not afraid to try and breach the flames, however fiercely they may burn.'

Charlotte instinctively drew back, afraid of the speed at which things were moving, and afraid, too, that she would betray her own emotions if he kissed her properly. So she gave him a cool look. 'Are you always this fast?'

He looked a little surprised, then grinned. 'But, Charlie, we've known each other for years!' It was impossible to go on being aloof and cold to him when he smiled at her like that. Her face relaxed into a smile and he said approvingly, 'That's better. You've turned off the ice.'

She laughed. 'I've an idea you've had a great deal of experience with women. Which puts me at a big disadvantage, doesn't it?'

'Does it?' His face grew intent. 'No, I don't think so, Charlie. I'm the one who's at a disadvantage. Because I've been waiting to meet someone like you for a long, long time.'

She gazed at him wide-eyed, taken aback by his sudden seriousness. She began to question it in her mind, wondering if it was just a line. But there was a lot of noise suddenly as horses began to be led towards the stables after another race, so Craig took her arm and quickly got out of the way, taking her back to the bar. But at the door he said, 'Are you still living at the Abbey?'

'Yes.'

'Then I'll come over and pick you up on Saturday. Will seven o'clock be all right?'

'Yes. Fine.'

Reaching out, he touched her hand lightly, his eyes smiling into hers. 'Till Saturday, then.'

He turned and walked away and Charlotte watched him go, feeling more than a little giddy. It had all happened so quickly. One moment it was just an ordinary pleasant day out with friends, and the next Craig was back in her life—and looked as if he meant to become a part of it. At least for a while. Because he was curious about her? Because he wanted to find out if she was as good in bed as Verity? That thought came unbidden into her mind and made Charlotte feel slightly sick. Why on earth should she think such a rotten thing of him? He had given her no indication at all that he had any deep memories of her sister, either good or bad. Luckily she recognised the emotion for what it was—jealousy. Jealousy of Verity, even after all these years. And not only because of Craig. Verity was quite famous now, and, although Charlotte didn't envy her sister's fame, she loathed being pointed out or introduced to people as 'the sister of Verity Page, the film star'.

'Charlotte?' Mike's voice behind her made her turn. 'Are you all right? We wondered where you'd got to.'

'Yes, I'm fine.' She managed a smile. 'Did you win anything on the last race?'

They went back into the bar to rejoin the Slaters and the day became ordinary again. Or at least on the surface. Beneath it Charlotte was bubbling with an inner excitement that she found hard to conceal. She tried to behave normally, but her thoughts were so full of Craig and what he'd said, and their coming date, that she often became abstracted and forgot to listen to the conversation, gazing into space and having to be brought back to reality. The Slaters laughed at her, but Tina gave her a shrewd look, and Mike, too, was in little doubt that her thoughts weren't on him.

Hartford Page never bothered to put himself out to meet Charlotte's friends, and she decided not to tell him that she'd met Craig. When Saturday came she was ready early and was sitting on the gate leading up to the Abbey when he arrived. He was driving a beautiful Porsche, but in a conservative dark blue colour. Which rather described Craig too, Charlotte thought as he got out of the car and walked towards her. He too was lean, powerful and easy on the eye, but was wearing a well-cut suit in a dark colour. Emotion threatened to overcome her, so she hid it by saying mockingly, 'Architecture must be on the up and up!'

He laughed. 'It usually is.' Coming to her, he looked up at her face for a long moment, then gave a small sigh and shook his head.

'What is it? Is something the matter with my face?'

'Yes. I've been telling myself that you couldn't have been as lovely as I remember, but you are, very much so.' And, putting his hands on her waist, he lifted her down and kissed her.

For a few moments Charlotte resisted him, but then she found that he didn't kiss her like most other men. His was neither the soft touch that left you completely unmoved, nor the automatic simulated passion that could be turned off like a car engine. Craig's kiss was warm and caressing, letting her know that he found her desirable but making no demands. Giving, exploring, tasting, arousing.

It wasn't a long kiss, as kisses went, but when he lifted his head Charlotte felt as if she'd taken a long voyage of discovery. She gave a sigh of pure pleasure. 'I *liked* that!'

'Well, thanks for the vote of confidence. We must do it again some time.'

She laughed rather breathlessly at that thought, and put her hand in his. 'I've met your horse, now introduce me to this mean machine.' And she indicated the car.

He did so with a touch of pride, pointing out all the gadgets and describing its performance as they drove along. He drove well, smooth and fast, with none of the over-steering round corners to show off that she'd encountered a couple of times with other men who'd fancied themselves as good drivers. But then, she thought, Craig had no need to show off, or any need to try and attract women. It was probably the other way round. Which made her wonder again why he'd asked her out. Was it because of how she was now—or because he was intrigued to find out if she was still in love with him?

After a while she said, 'You drive well, and you ride well. Are you a good architect too?'

He gave her a quick glance before looking back at the road. 'What a question! Now how am I supposed to answer that? I try to be. But I'm learning all the time. Every plan you draw is different. And you have to try to please so many people—the companies, the economists, the environmentalists.' He shrugged. 'Sometimes you just can't win and, what's worse, you know it from the very start, which is discouraging. But every now and again things go right and you build something that is really worth while. *That's* when you get real job satisfaction and feel that it's all been worth it.'

'Like riding Blanico past the winning post?' Charlotte said softly.

Craig smiled, almost to himself, his lips twitching. 'Yes, that—and one or two other things.'

Charlotte wisely didn't ask what. But she really didn't have to. She was coming to realise that Craig strove for perfection in all that he did. And, if that kiss was anything to go by, he would be quite something as a lover, too. She flushed a little at her own thoughts and quickly began to talk of other things, but was well aware that Craig knew exactly what she'd been thinking.

She had a marvellous time that night, sitting with Craig in a candlelit restaurant, eating food that she knew was good but unaware of what she actually ate, talking animatedly or listening intently, her chin propped on her hand, her eyes fixed on his face. And he seemed to be just as engrossed in her, drawing her out and laughing at her dry wit, sparring with her on some subjects and on others in complete agreement. Charlotte forgot about the other people in the room, forgot the time and even forgot that Verity had found Craig first. In fact Verity wasn't mentioned at all and her father only once, when Craig said that he hadn't noticed any new books by him recently and enquired how he was.

'Oh, he's fine, thanks.' Charlotte hesitated. 'Well, actually, no, he's not. Not as far as his writing's concerned, anyway. He still shuts himself away in his study every day, but he doesn't seem to produce anything. When I ask him about it he just mutters about ''writer's block''.'

'And how long has this been going on?'

'A few years now.'

'That's a shame. And it must make things a bit difficult for you.'

'Not really. As a matter of fact, we don't see a great deal of each other. I go out quite a lot, and if I take anyone back he just escapes to his study.'

'I seem to remember he was sociable enough before.'

'Yes, he used to be,' Charlotte admitted. 'But he's changed.' She didn't see any point in telling Craig that it had always been Verity's friends that her father had welcomed; Charlotte's he thought too ordinary and uninteresting. Mostly because they weren't in show business or weren't creative. Computer programmers and accountants held no interest for him, regardless of their personalities.

'Is he working on a book now?'

'Oh, yes. He's always working on one—he just never seems to be able to finish it. Perhaps he's just written himself out.'

Deliberately she changed the subject then, telling Craig about the horse she'd borrowed from the Slaters.

Reaching for her hand under the table, Craig smiled at her. 'Tell you what, how would you like to go out riding with me? I've a friend who trains horses, steeple-chasers mostly. I often go to help exercise the horses and I'm sure he could find something suitable for you. His wife rides a lot too, so you could probably borrow her horse.'

'I'd love that,' Charlotte enthused, her grey eyes lighting. 'And could we go round the stables?'

'Ah, you want to meet Blanico again, do you?'

'Is that where he's kept?'

'Mm.' He leant towards her. 'If you ask me nicely, I might be able to fix it.'

She gave him a mock wary look. 'How nicely?'

'Oh, very, very nicely.'

She wrinkled her nose. 'Oh, in that case...'

'I give in,' he said instantly, lifting his free hand open palm towards her. 'If Blanico can't tempt you, then I know I'm in a losing battle.' His hand tightened on hers and he looked at her warmly. 'Do you know you have freckles on your nose?'

'Of course. How cruel of you to remind me!'

'Don't be silly, they're delightful. One day I'm going to count them.'

Charlotte laughed. 'It will probably take all day.'

'Good.' His eyes darkened. 'And then I'm going to kiss them, one by one.' He raised his eyebrows, his eyes sending teasing messages. 'Do you think that might take all night?'

But she refused to be drawn and said lightly, 'I've always thought you grew out of freckles, but I seem to be stuck with them. At school I used to go to bed with slices of lemon on my face because someone told me that got rid of them.'

'And did it make any difference?'

'No, but I always smelt very fresh in the morning.'

Craig burst into laughter, the sound of his genuine amusement causing many heads to turn and look at them. 'And do you still do it?'

'Oh, no, I gave up years ago. I've learnt to live with them by now.'

'Good,' he said, and gave her a mocking, enigmatic smile. 'Lemon slices might just be a little off-putting.'

And make of that what you may, Charlotte thought with a quickening heart.

They left the restaurant and walked for a while in the soft April night, hand in hand, talking a little, sometimes laughing, sometimes just strolling in a contented silence. After a while it grew colder and they retraced their steps back to the car, but Charlotte found herself walking slowly, not wanting the evening to end. Craig glanced at her, let go of her hand and instead put his arm round her waist, holding her near so that she could feel his leanness against her. 'Cold?' he asked.

'No, not really.'

'I thought you shivered.'

'No, I—I didn't shiver.'

His arm tightened a little and his lips lightly brushed her hair. Charlotte felt a great surge of desire. She wanted him to stop and take her in his arms, to kiss and caress her, a longing so urgent that another great tremor of awareness ran through her. Craig must have felt it and he seemed to understand, but he did nothing until he had driven her home and they got out of the car at the gate leading to the Abbey. By then Charlotte had belatedly remembered that this was only their first date and she ought to hold back, to keep Craig at a distance.

But that was easier resolved than carried out. Taking her hand, he opened the gate and began to walk with her along the drive beneath the dappled shadow of trees coming into bud.

'You really don't have to come all the way up to the house with me,' Charlotte protested nervously.

'No?' He stopped, and for a terrifying moment she thought he was going to take her at her word. But then he drew her to him and held her close, moulding her body against his. 'Here, then,' he said softly, and kissed her.

It was the most sensuous experience Charlotte had ever known. Her body seemed to melt against his, consumed by the fierce flame of desire he lit within her. There was nothing else in the world but his lips and his body hard against hers. There was no power of resistance left, only an overwhelming yearning to be closer and closer still. It was at once gratifying and frustrating; wonderful to be held and kissed but creating a longing for fulfilment that grew with every jumping heartbeat.

Raising his head at last, Craig held her against his shoulder, his face against her hair. For a few moments she fought to control her breathing, but then Craig lifted his hand and laid it lightly on her breast, feeling the wild beating of her heart. Charlotte quickly looked up at him, trying to read his features, but his face was in shadow. He took his hand away and gently pushed her hair back from her hot skin, then lightly kissed her on the forehead before walking on again towards the house.

Charlotte knew she was lost. In her heart she had gone on loving him all these years, and when he had reappeared, even more arrantly masculine and attractive than she remembered, any reluctance she might have felt had withered away into nothing. Especially after the way he had singled her out—and that even before he knew who she was. No, given the past and the emotions he aroused in her now, Charlotte hadn't a hope of resisting anything he wanted of her.

She was still clinging to him as they came out of the trees into the piece of open ground in front of the bridge. Craig bent to kiss her again as they walked and their steps gradually slowed until they stood still concentrating only on each other.

'When can I see you again?' he demanded thickly, his mouth exploring her neck.

'Well, I don't know, I...'

'Tomorrow,' he said fiercely. 'And the next day and the next. Say yes, Charlie. Please say yes!'

Her voice shaking, she said, 'All right, tomorrow.'

He hugged her tightly, almost hurting her, and drew her across the bridge into the deep, cool shadows of the gatehouse. There they kissed again for a long time before he at last tore himself away.

'Till tomorrow, then,' he said raggedly. 'I'll pick you up at ten-thirty.'

'Yes, all right.' She followed him to the bridge, then called, 'Craig!'

'Yes?' He turned to look back at her, a tall, heart-stopping figure in the silver moonlight.

'Just—be careful,' she answered lamely, because her heart was too full to find any other words.

But he understood. 'Always,' he assured her. 'Always—now.' And then he turned and was running back to his car. Running with the joyous lightness of youth and well-being.

Charlotte watched him go, watched until even the keenest of ears could no longer hear the sound of the Porsche's engine echoing through the night, but she still didn't go in. She just leaned against the bridge and looked mistily into a possible future that held nothing but the golden glow of happiness and love.

CHAPTER THREE

THAT SPRING was the most wonderful time Charlotte had ever known. From that day her life revolved completely around Craig. Even when she wasn't with him, her heart and mind was full of him, and everything else in her life was merely incidental. During the week, when she was at work, she looked out for amusing or interesting things to tell him, and if she went shopping for clothes it was always with whether he would like it in mind, or whether he had admired her in a certain colour. In the evenings she rushed home from work, even though it might be hours before he rang, wishing they didn't live so far apart so that they could meet more often. But with Craig working at an exacting job in London that often kept him at the office until late, and also meant that he had to go away on frequent business trips, there was really only the weekends when they could see each other.

Once, though, Craig had rung her at work and said that he would be in her area that afternoon; could she get away early and meet him? Charlotte had immediately gone to her boss and asked for the time off. Her request had surprised him, especially as she gave neither an excuse nor an explanation. She was always so conscientious that he would have given it to her anyway, but there was a determination in her voice that told him not to refuse or she would just walk out. He remarked on this, jokingly, and Charlotte's eyes widened in surprise as she realised that he was right. A job that she valued and her hard-won position in the company were suddenly completely unimportant any more. But the fact that her values had changed so quickly and so irreversibly caused only a moment's wonder and was then accepted without question. Craig was once again the most important part of her life.

And her happiness showed. As she began to go out with Craig regularly, Charlotte's inner radiance gave her a glow of eager vitality that made her look lovelier than she ever had before. She had always taken a proper pride in her appearance, but now she took extra care, wanting Craig to be proud of her, and her mirror told her how she sparkled.

Craig soon got in the habit of calling her every evening, even when he was away, and Charlotte ran to answer the phone, forgetting everything else, so that washing-up water grew cold, the iron got left on, and the television set played to an empty room for an hour at a time. Renate remonstrated at first, then philosophically made sure that whatever Charlotte was using when the phone rang was switched off. Their conversations were long, there always seemed so much to talk about, and Charlotte would picture Craig in his London flat, or stretched out on the bed in some hotel room, and wish they were together. And Craig must have felt the same, because he demanded to know where she was and what she was doing, and often said he missed her. Staying in every evening to wait for his call didn't do much for her social life, but Charlotte didn't care, she lived for those phone calls and for the weekends when they could be together.

As soon as he could arrange it, Craig took her to his friend's stables, as he'd promised. He picked her up early one Saturday morning when the mist was still on the ground, and they drove across country, westwards along the motorway until they reached the Berkshire Downs. Craig's friends, Nigel and Amanda Hoylake, came to the door of their red-brick Victorian house to welcome them, both already dressed for riding. They were in their mid to late thirties and seemed to be on good terms with Craig, who greeted them warmly, shaking Nigel's hand and giving Amanda an affectionate kiss.

Amanda returned the kiss with equal warmth and turned to greet Charlotte, giving her a very feminine once-over as she did so. 'Hello. How nice to meet you.'

They went into the Hoylakes' big kitchen for a stand-up cup of coffee while they chatted a little, the two men talking easily together and the two women making small talk as they sized each other up. But it seemed that Amanda approved, because she put a friendly hand on Charlotte's arm as she indicated which way to go when they went out to the stables. Craig was given a spirited gelding to ride, which pleased him, and Charlotte a beautiful chestnut mare that came eagerly to the door for a carrot when she saw them.

'You're honoured,' Craig told her. 'That's the horse Amanda sometimes rides in point-to-points.'

The Hoylakes came with them and Charlotte felt very much as if her horsemanship was under scrutiny, but she was as competent as any girl who had ridden nearly all her life, and although the horse she had been given was of a much better quality than she'd been used to, she soon felt at ease and thoroughly enjoyed the ride. But then with Craig beside her how could she be anything else but happy? They went sedately at first through the outskirts of the village, but, when they reached the long, green stretch of the Downs, let the horses have their heads. Charlotte gave a cry of delight, loving every minute. Craig thundered along beside her, keeping pace, making sure she was all right on this, the first time he had ever seen her ride. Then he too laughed and started to make a race of it, so that she knew he had stopped worrying about her.

Those twenty minutes or so of their gallop were among the most exhilarating in Charlotte's life. To have a good horse under her, the wind in her face, and Craig beside her—Charlotte felt that must be very close to heaven, and when at last they slowed to a walk, she thanked her hosts warmly.

Amanda smiled at her glowing face. 'It was fun, wasn't it?' And to Craig, 'You must bring Charlie over again.'

That day was a race day, and the Hoylakes had two horses entered for a meeting that afternoon, one of which Craig was riding, so they went back to the stables to make sure everything was in order, leaving Craig and Charlotte to follow more slowly.

'We have an hour or so yet,' Craig told her. 'Let's head over to that piece of woodland.'

They walked the horses over, letting them cool down, and avoiding the strings of horses that were still out exercising, although most of them had gone back to their stables by now.

'I can see why you love this,' Charlotte enthused. 'It's a perfect setting. And that ride was marvellous!'

'It's always been my ambition to own a house here,' Craig replied. 'Oh, nothing lavish. Perhaps just a holiday cottage, so that I could come down here and at least watch the horses, even if I couldn't get a ride.'

'And are you going to? Are you looking round for a place?'

He shook his head regretfully. 'It will have to wait, I'm afraid. You know how busy I am in the partnership—trying to set up your own business takes up a hell of a lot of time. And having two homes for only one person does seem over-indulgent.'

Charlotte nodded, remembering that Craig, along with two older colleagues, had decided to branch out on their own only a couple of years ago and were putting all their efforts into building up their name and business.

'Both of my partners are married, of course,' Craig added. 'Which puts the onus on to me a little when it comes to taking jobs abroad or away from London.' He came to the trees and slowed to a walk, turned to give her a smile that caught at her heart. 'But from now on I think that I'm going to insist that I have every weekend free to see you.'

They walked a little way into the wood until the Downs were hidden by the trees. Taking the reins from her, Craig tied the horses to a low branch, then turned and opened his arms. 'Come here,' he commanded huskily.

Charlotte went to him gladly, putting her arms around his neck and returning his kiss without reserve.

'I've missed you,' he murmured against her mouth, his lips avid for hers. 'A whole week without seeing you is too long, too long.'

Charlotte couldn't have agreed with him more and proved it by the way she responded, her mouth opening under his as she clung to him, her body held close as he put his hands low on her hips. Craig's shoulders hunched as the kiss deepened into passion, but then he groaned and straightened up. 'Oh, Charlie! Oh, Charlie.'

'What? What is it?'

'Oh, I think you know.' His eyes, still dark with desire, looked into hers. 'You turn me on, sweetheart. You have from the first moment I met you.'

'The *first* moment?' Charlotte questioned, lifting a finger to run it along his lips.

'Mm? Oh, I see what you mean. Well, no, not quite then. I meant since I met you again at Sandown.'

Charlotte smiled but drew back a little. No, she definitely hadn't turned him on when they'd met six years ago, because then his thoughts had been full of Verity. It had been her sister he'd wanted, who he hadn't been able to take his eyes off, who he'd held and kissed.

She looked down and stepped back, but Craig reached out for her again. 'Hey, what's the matter?'

'Nothing. Why should there be?' But she didn't meet his eyes.

'Am I going too fast for you, is that it?' he asked with a frown between his dark brows.

'No. No, of course not.' Determinedly she pushed the past out of her mind. It was the here and now that mattered, and Craig had just said that he had fallen for her the first moment they met again. What more could a girl want? And she smiled as she went back into his arms, kissing him with a fierce hunger as if she would force the past back where it belonged, in deep oblivion.

Sometimes, of course, Craig drove down from London after work to take her out. Usually then they went out to dinner at a local restaurant, but Charlotte would always wait for him at the gate, never at the house, even if it was raining, running forward when he arrived, laughing and happy as he hugged and kissed her as if they'd been apart for months instead of days. After Charlotte had repaired her lipstick they would drive to the place they'd chosen and eat unhurriedly, enjoying being together in this intimacy among strangers, their hands sometimes touching, and their eyes meeting to pass messages that made her heart swell with love and a warm sense of continuous excitement.

Only small things happened to wake her from this euphoric state, but they were enough to mar her happiness, for a while at least. Because they often went to local restaurants, it was inevitable that Charlotte sometimes met people she knew. Usually this didn't matter in the least, and she was more than proud to introduce Craig to them, but once they had run into one of the directors of her firm who had taken his wife and daughter out to dinner to celebrate the daughter's eighteenth birthday. He introduced Charlotte to them, and as soon as the girl heard Charlotte's surname she exclaimed, 'Oh, then surely you must be the sister of Verity Page, the actress. I read in a film magazine that she came from this area.'

Charlotte acknowledged the relationship briefly and tried to change the subject, but the girl unfortunately turned out to be a fan of Verity's and started asking lots of questions. Her parents looked on dotingly, expecting Charlotte to be pleased at having this secondhand claim to fame recognised, but she was getting more and more uptight with every eager question and might have ended up curtly cutting the girl off if the waitress hadn't come up to tell the family that their table was ready. 'Won't you join us?' the father offered hospitably. 'You'd be very welcome.'

'Thank you, but no,' Charlotte said firmly, with an inward shudder at the thought of hearing Verity's name thrown at her all evening.

They nodded and went away, leaving Charlotte to sit back in her chair with a sigh of relief, but she was still stiff with tension and only too aware that Craig had also been reminded of Verity. She finished her drink too quickly and tried to think of something safe to say, but for the moment everything else was driven from her mind, and it was Craig who spoke first.

'It doesn't sound as if you hear from Verity very often?'

'No.' Charlotte would have liked to leave it there, but he raised an enquiring eyebrow and she felt compelled to add, 'I think my father hears from her now and again.'

'But he doesn't tell you?' There was astonishment in Craig's tone.

The truth was that Charlotte never asked her father if he'd had a letter from Verity, firstly because if he hadn't heard for some time it upset him, and if he had he would bring out the letter anyway and read it aloud, making comments about how well Verity was doing and what fascinating people she was mixing with. Uttering paeans of praise for his far-away daughter—the daughter who sent only two or three letters a year, and never rang or came back to visit him. He would then look at Charlotte, who was near enough keeping a roof over his head, shake his head and wish she could have an interesting life like her sister's! Goaded into rashness, Charlotte had once suggested that he visit Verity in America, and the idea had so pleased him that her father had gone straight to his study to pass the suggestion on to his elder daughter. Charlotte had immediately felt remorseful, but even more so when the weeks passed and Verity didn't reply, not getting in touch again until the next Christmas when she sent a card which didn't even mention the proposed visit. Hartford Page had never said anything about it, but his shoulders seemed to sag a little more afterwards, and Charlotte felt terrible about it.

Now she shook her head in answer to Craig's question. 'We don't talk about Verity very much. As a matter of fact,' she added awkwardly, 'he doesn't talk about anything very much—he spends most of the time in his study.'

'That must be lonely for you,' Craig remarked, putting out a hand to cover hers.

She smiled and turned her hand under his, glad of its warmth and strength. 'No, I'm not lonely,' she said softly. She didn't add, 'not now', she didn't need to, it was there in her face for all to see.

But then Craig spoiled it all again by saying, 'I read in the paper that Verity's in a new film that's opening in the West End soon. Would you like to go and see it? If you like we could really make a night of it and go to the première.'

Charlotte's hand tensed under his and she drew it away. 'It's sweet of you to suggest it,' she began, then floundered, 'but I... but I...'

'Well?' he laughed. 'But what?'

'But I never go to watch Verity's films,' Charlotte got out abruptly.

'You don't? Why ever not? It would be different if it was a stage production and you were afraid of bringing her bad luck or something, but a film has already been shot ages ago; you going to see it could hardly put a jinx on it now,' Craig pointed out, a mildly surprised look in his dark eyes.

'It's not that. I... Oh, my glass is empty. Could I have another drink, please?'

'Of course.' Craig beckoned the bar waiter over, but then turned back to her. There was an intent look in his eyes that made Charlotte's heart sink, and she was right, for he immediately said, 'Well, come on, why don't you go and see Verity's films? And it doesn't sound as if you write to her, either.'

'I'd rather not talk about it, OK?' she answered shortly.

Craig was silent for a moment as he looked at her flushed cheeks, then sat back in his chair. 'As you wish.'

He was silent then, a silence that grew and to Charlotte became taut with unspoken questions, until in the end she couldn't stand it any longer and turned to face him, snapping out, 'Look, you had an almighty row with Verity and walked out on her yourself. Isn't it possible that I could have had a row with her, too?'

'More than possible,' Craig agreed. 'But just when did you two have this fight? She's been in the States for over five years, hasn't she? Oh, but of course—she must have been home to visit since then.'

'No.' Charlotte shook her head. 'She's never been back.'

She was sitting very straight and tense, her face pale except for the spots of high colour on her cheekbones. Craig gave her a puzzled look, but wisely changed the subject, watching with interest as she soon became her normal, happy self again.

After their evenings spent having dinner together, Craig would drive slowly back to the Abbey, both of them reluctant for the night to end, and when they reached it they would stand in the shadow of the gate-house to say goodnight or, if it was cold, sit in the warm but cramped confines of Craig's car.

It was on one of the latter nights when it was blowing almost a gale outside that Craig drew back from kissing her and said wryly, 'This damn car was never meant to say goodnight in.'

'You could always get a large saloon,' Charlotte chuckled as he rubbed his ribs where the gear lever had been pressing.

'Or you might even ask me into the house,' he countered rather pointedly. 'Or is it the tradition in these rural parts that you have to go out with a girl for a set length of time before she asks you in?'

Charlotte hesitated, her face a picture of warring emotions in the dim light of the car, but then she realised that it was hardly being fair on Craig to treat him like this. She couldn't expect to keep him and her father apart for ever, much as she would have liked to, and it *was* awfully cold. So they went into the house to find that Hartford Page had already gone to bed and they had the sitting-room to themselves. They put more logs on the fire until it crackled and flamed, then pulled up the settee and turned down the lights—and it wasn't until gone one in the morning before Craig reluctantly tore himself away to drive back to London.

From then on he usually came into the house to say goodnight and almost always her father had already gone up to his room, or went there straight from his study, but one evening a few weeks later he found that he had left a book in the sitting-room and, when he came down to get it, found them there.

Charlotte moved quickly away from where she was sitting close to Craig on the settee, but he got easily to his feet and held out his hand to her father. 'Hello, sir. I'm Craig Bishop. We did meet once before, but it was a very long time ago.'

'Really?' The older man took his hand and looked at him without much interest. 'I'm afraid I can't quite recall ... Did Charlie bring you?'

'No, Charlie was just a schoolgirl then,' Craig said with a grin in her direction. 'No, actually I came with Verity.'

'With Verity?' Hartford Page immediately lifted his head to look at him more closely. 'Why, yes, I think I do remember now. Aren't you an architect or something in that line? Good lord, it *was* a long time ago! Verity's been gone for several years, you know.' An idea came to him and he said eagerly, 'I say, you haven't seen her, have you? Is that why you're here? Did she give you some messages for me?'

'No, I'm afraid not,' Craig said gently. 'I haven't seen her myself since I was last here. I'm with Charlie,' he explained as the other man frowned in perplexity.

'Oh, I see—Charlie.' Her father looked disappointed, then brightened. 'Well, as you're a friend of Verity's, I've got something that I'm sure you'd very much like to see. Just you wait a moment.'

He went over to the bookcase and Charlotte's heart sank, knowing what was coming. He now had a press-cuttings book for Verity into which he assiduously put all her press notices, sent to him by an agency they could ill afford to pay, plus the few items she sent to him herself. He loved to show this off to people, but his own press-cuttings book was sadly seldom opened now, either to put in new entries or to show to visitors.

He brought the binder over and told Charlotte to move to a chair so that he could sit next to Craig and go through the book with him. She obeyed silently, deliberately avoiding the swift glance Craig threw her. Then she had to sit and endure a whole hour of undiluted Verity; her beauty, her talent, her star quality, her film star friends, her past, present and future films. Hartford Page had her whole career at his fingertips, and to hear him talk Verity must have been the hottest property in the film world, instead of just another actress struggling to make a name for herself. She did have some talent, Charlotte had to admit that, but so did thousands of other aspiring starlets, and 'some' just wasn't enough without a great deal of luck or influence to go with it.

Craig was very good; he sat patiently beside the older man, listening, making the right comments, and appearing to be genuinely interested. If he wasn't, if he was wishing they could be left alone, he certainly didn't show it. If Charlotte hadn't remembered the hunger with which he'd started to kiss her before they were interrupted, she would have thought he was far more fascinated by the endless details of Verity's career. At first he had tried to draw Charlotte into the conversation, but she answered only in monosyllables, and after giving her an assessing look he had left her alone and concentrated on the cuttings.

They came to the end at last, with even her father unable to find anything else to say, and he reluctantly rose to his feet. 'Well, I'd better be getting up to bed—a full day's writing to do tomorrow, you know. You must get Charlie to bring you again, Craig. I'm sure I'll have lots more cuttings to show you after Verity's new film opens. Come then. Come then. Well, goodnight.'

He put the book back on to its shelf in the bookcase and went out. The room was suddenly very empty, and very quiet again, but not peaceful, not any more.

'Why don't you come and sit over here?' Craig suggested, indicating the place where her father had sat beside him.

Charlotte hesitated a moment, then went over, but as she sat down said stiltedly, 'It's getting very late; don't you think you ought to be starting back?'

'Trying to get rid of me?' Craig put an arm round her shoulders and drew her close to him.

'No.' She spoke reluctantly, but he began to kiss her earlobe, and after a moment she suddenly turned to face him and put her arms round his neck, her eyes vulnerable. 'No, I don't ever want to get rid of you.' And she kissed him fiercely, trying to shut out the last hour, trying to reassure herself that *she* was the one Craig was interested in.

And he reciprocated so satisfactorily that neither of them had time for words for quite some time. But at length he lifted his head to smile down at her as she lay across his lap, her eyes soft and languorous, her mouth still parted from the passion of his kisses.

'I don't want to leave,' he said regretfully.

'I don't want you to either.' Charlotte turned her head to kiss his hand and he gently stroked her cheek. 'I'd ask you to stay but,' her voice hardened, 'I'm afraid my father... Well, he seems to have a one-track mind these days.'

'You mean he'd keep on about Verity? He does seem to have rather an obsession about her. But he's obviously very proud of her.'

'He's always been obsessed with her,' Charlotte said shortly. She sat up and began to do up her blouse.

'Hey, that's my job!' Craig bent to kiss the valley between her breasts one last time before doing up the buttons, so slowly that Charlotte was tingling with awareness again before he'd finished. But as he did up the last one he said, 'Are you jealous of your father's interest in Verity?'

Charlotte could have said a whole lot, but it was late and she wanted to stay warm in the memory of Craig's lovemaking, not have to think of her sister again. Anyway, she was used to being the unfavoured daughter and didn't care so much any more because she'd found Craig, so she just said, 'No, not if it keeps him happy.' But she stood up, putting an end to the conversation as she helped him into his coat. One last kiss at the door and then the evening was over at last.

But after that things weren't so pleasant, because now her father sometimes made a point of waiting up for her to come home so that he could talk to Craig again. And always Verity's name would come into it; even if Craig started talking about something else, Hartford Page would always manage to twist the conversation back to Verity. If it hadn't been for that Charlotte would have been pleased that her father was being sociable with one of her friends. But then, in his eyes, Craig wasn't her friend at all; Verity had brought him, so he would always remain Verity's friend.

And, as time went on and Charlotte fell even deeper in love with Craig, a tiny doubt that had always been in her mind began to grow as she wondered if her father was right. It wasn't that she had any real doubts about how Craig felt about *her*, but she began to wonder more and more just how deeply Craig had felt for Verity— and whether he still had any feelings for her now. Little things made it grow; a chance remark that she reminded him of Verity when she pouted, his willingness to talk of Verity with her father, and the fact that Craig had gone to see Verity's latest film without telling her. This she only found out when Hartford Page was talking enthusiastically about the film—which he'd made a special journey to London to see—and Craig mentioned that he'd already seen it.

Stupid things. But they niggled at her mind so that sometimes she was a little thoughtful, a little restrained, as she watched Craig and wondered if he'd ever taken Verity to his favourite Italian restaurant in Soho, had bought her yellow roses, and had held her and kissed her too until the world spun round—or had ever taken her to bed and made love to her. Had he? Had he? Had he?

Most of the time she managed to banish such disturbing thoughts to the back of her mind, but they would return suddenly, awakened against her will and spoiling her happiness. She tried very hard to hide all this from Craig, and she largely succeeded, but it preyed on her mind so much that she couldn't conceal it entirely.

'Hey,' he chided her one day when something had happened to make her think of him and Verity together, 'you've got that look on your face again.'

She turned to him in surprise. 'What look?'

'A kind of closed-in look, as if you're thinking of something unpleasant. What were you thinking of?'

'Oh, nothing. It doesn't matter.'

It was a Saturday morning and they were walking in London's Hyde Park alongside the Serpentine, watching the ducks gather on the sun-dappled water, but now Craig stopped and turned her round to face him, his hands on her shoulders. He looked at her searchingly, then said, 'Charlie, have I done something to upset you?'

'Why, no, of course not.'

'Then why are you shutting me out?' he asked bluntly.

'I'm not. I . . .' She broke off and then flushed as she saw him raise his eyebrows. She sighed and looked at him uncertainly, not wanting to tell him of her fears.

But Craig's hands tightened on her shoulders and he said sternly, 'Whatever it is, Charlie, don't you think I have a right to know? It's been troubling you for some time, hasn't it?'

Charlotte gave a little groan. 'Oh, dear, I thought I'd managed to hide it. I—I didn't want to tell you, it's so— so petty.'

'Hardly petty when it makes you look at me sometimes as if I was a stranger. So tell me, Charlie,' he commanded in a tone that implied he wasn't to be put off.

'Well, all right, but you're—you're going to think I'm being stupid, I know,' she said reluctantly.

'Try me.' Craig took her hand and led her over to a wooden bench alongside the pathway. They sat down and he put an arm across her shoulders, looking directly into her face. 'Now,' he commanded. 'And don't leave anything out.'

'OK.' Charlotte gave him a rueful look, wishing he wouldn't look at her so closely, and wondering if her fears would disgust him or whether he would just find them ludicrous. Of the two, she decided, she would probably prefer the latter. Slowly she said, 'There is something on my mind, something I can't shut out, no matter how hard I try. And I *have* tried, Craig, please believe that. I know it shouldn't matter, but it does, and I...'

'All right, I can see that,' Craig broke in on her agitation. 'So, tell me.'

'Well—it's Verity. You and Verity.'

'Ah, I'm beginning to understand.' He drew back a little and she looked anxiously into his face, searching it for some sign of the effect her admission had had on him, but his features were completely unreadable. 'So, what about me and Verity?'

His voice had hardened and she became frightened again, but it was too late to turn back now. 'I keep thinking about—about the two of you together.' He was silent, waiting for her to go on, but she turned away as she said, 'And I can't help wondering how—how you felt about her.'

'I see. You're worrying your head about something that happened over six years ago.'

She turned to look at him. '*Did* something happen?'

His brows flickered and there was a rather wry twist to his lips, but he neither laughed nor frowned. 'You mean did we go to bed together,' he said bluntly.

Charlotte stiffened. 'Yes, I suppose I do.'

'And is it going to make any difference to us?'

She stared at him, her eyes wide as he came straight out with the question she had never dared to ask herself. But now, faced with it, her answer was instinctive. 'No. But—but I'd feel a hell of a lot better if I knew you hadn't,' she admitted honestly.

Craig grinned at her and moved his hand to her neck. 'Then you can start right now, because the answer's no, I never made love to Verity.'

'You didn't?' Charlotte's eyes lit with relief. 'Not even once?''

He laughed and gave her a gentle shake. 'Not even once. Verity knew how to play very hard to get.'

She looked at him searchingly. 'And you weren't in love with her?'

'In love? No. No, I don't think so.' Craig's eyes became withdrawn, as if he was looking back into the past. 'I remember I was extremely attracted to her; she was very lovely even then.'

'And you wanted her?' Charlotte said hollowly.

His eyes rose to her face. 'Yes, I wanted her. I wanted her very badly. And I was inexperienced enough then to be a willing fish on her hook—at first. But then I found out that she was going around with other men at the same time, and I came to my senses enough to realise that the game wasn't worth the candle, so I opted out.'

At the mention of other men, Charlotte's face had suffused with colour and she quickly turned away. 'But—but if there hadn't been other men, would you have gone on?'

'Possibly. Probably, I suppose. Why?'

She couldn't answer, could only shake her head miserably.

'Are you thinking of that night at the Abbey when Verity and I split up?' She nodded dumbly and he continued, 'That night you lied your head off about Verity's string of lovers?'

Charlotte turned to stare at him, bug-eyed. 'You *knew*?'

He laughed aloud. 'Of course I knew. You were a rotten liar.' His face sobered. 'But there was an element of truth in it for all that. And put together with what I'd learnt about Verity in London—well, it made me damn angry to think how she'd been stringing me along.'

'Oh, God, what a relief! All these years I've been afraid I was the cause of you two breaking up,' Charlotte admitted. 'Not that I didn't want you to split, but I still felt responsible.'

'You were, though, in a way. When I compared you, so young and untouched, and so willing to declare how you felt, with Verity's cat and mouse games, it made me see how she was trying to use me. She sickened me,' he said with a cold look of remembrance.

'So you had a fight.'

'I told her we were through, yes. She wasn't very happy about it.'

Charlotte remembered the way Verity had hit her afterwards and mentally agreed with him. But then she frowned and said, 'Did you tell Verity that *I'd* told you?'

'No, of course not.' Craig shook his head decisively.

'But she knew. She accused me of breaking you up.'

'Did she?' He frowned, trying to remember. 'I was so damn angry... Wait a minute, didn't you mention something about a neighbour Verity was stringing along, too? Yes, I remember I threw that at her, and she must have realised that only you could have told me. Yes, sorry, I'm afraid that must have been it.'

Charlotte nodded, but her eyes were on his face as she said, 'If you were that angry then you must have been—quite emotionally involved,' she said with slow reluctance.

Craig returned her look steadily. 'I've already admitted that I wanted her—up until that night.' He reached out to touch her cheek. 'The night I met you. Maybe it happened even then,' he said softly.

'What happened?' Charlotte found it suddenly difficult to breathe.

He smiled and bent to kiss the tip of her nose and his eyes darkened. 'Do you have to go home tonight?' he asked, his voice suddenly thickening. 'Couldn't you stay?'

'Stay? You mean—with you?' Charlotte's throat tightened as she gazed at him.

'Of course with me.'

Her heart began to thump crazily and for a moment she couldn't speak, but then she nodded and somehow managed to say, 'Yes, I... All right.'

'Good.' He bent to kiss her lightly, his eyes holding hers, dark with anticipation, but as he raised his head a roguish look came into them, and he said, 'I have a very comfortable couch in the sitting-room you can sleep on!'

Charlotte punched him in the ribs and he burst out laughing, but then sprang to his feet and pulled her up beside him to wrap her in a tight bear-hug and kiss her just as exuberantly. 'Oh, Charlie, Charlie, Charlie. I hope you don't choose that couch tonight.'

'Certainly I shall,' she retorted. 'You deserve to be punished.'

He still held her tightly, but his eyebrows rose as he looked at her. 'Playing cat and mouse?' he asked with a wry look in his eyes.

'No.' She shook her head in sharp sincerity. 'No, I'll never do that. I'm me—not Verity.'

'And are you happy now—about her and me?'

'Yes. Thank you.'

He kissed her again and she knew she would never have to worry about Verity any more, that anxiety was dead and buried for ever. She felt so safe now, so content in his arms. And tonight she would be truly his—as Verity had never been.

'It's only eleven o'clock, what do you want to do for the rest of the day?'

'Oh, there's always so much to do in London. But if—if I'm staying overnight then I'll have to phone

Renate and tell her, otherwise she'll worry. And I'll have to give her your number in case of emergency, I'm afraid. She always insists on that whenever I go away.'

The rest of that day passed in a hazy kind of dream. Charlotte knew that they went to an antique market and a picture gallery, and afterwards had dinner on a restaurant boat that cruised along the Grand Union Canal which went right through the heart of London Zoo. The atmosphere was warm and friendly; Craig toasted her silently, his eyes holding hers over his glass of wine, and there was an accordionist who soon had everyone joining in his songs. A perfect night that Charlotte knew would be the most memorable of her life. The boat turned at Little Venice and glided through a tunnel so that Charlotte could see their reflections in the window glass, looking at them as if they were two different people and liking what she saw. Craig, so broad and handsome, a smouldering look of desire in his dark eyes. And herself, so bright and vibrant, her eyes large and expectant as she thought of the night to come. Craig followed her glance and smiled in immediate understanding. He took her hand and leaned forward, his eyes very intent. He started to say, 'Charlie, my darling girl, I...' but the accordionist broke into a loud and jingling tune behind him and he gave a rueful grin and shook his head. 'Later,' he mouthed, and Charlotte nodded, her heart tight in her chest at the wild hope that he was going to ask her to marry him.

It was almost midnight when they reached Craig's flat. He turned the key in the lock and smiled at her as he pushed the door open. He went to take her hand to draw her inside, but then heard the phone ringing and his eyebrows rose in surprise. With a muttered apology he hurried into the sitting-room to answer it, and Charlotte followed, shutting the door behind her.

But as she stepped into the room Craig held the receiver out towards her. 'It's for you. It's Renate.'

She gave him a mystified look and took it from him, said hello and then stood, her face draining of colour as she listened to the housekeeper. She said, 'Where?' in a strange, strangled voice and after another few moments slowly put down the phone, her hand shaking.

'Darling, what is it? What's happened?' Craig asked urgently.

'It's—it's my father. He's had a stroke. Oh, Craig, they don't know whether he's going to live!'

CHAPTER FOUR

THE DRIVE down to the Abbey from London seemed to be endless. Charlotte sat in silence, her eyes on the dark ribbon of the road, wondering what the future held for her. Would her father recover, or would he be an invalid whom she and Renate would have to care for for the rest of his life? If Renate would stay on. She didn't like nursing and had a very abrupt bedside manner, to say the least. A chill feeling entered Charlotte's heart as she realised that she might have to give up work, or at least take a part-time job. And how they would then manage financially she hated to even think about. The house would have to go, of course, if they could find anyone to buy it. But it had been so neglected lately that they might not get very much for it. And, if she did have to look after her father, what then of her relationship with Craig? Charlotte shivered and looked ahead at a suddenly bleak future, the contrast to her happiness a few hours ago making it even more marked. But her father's welfare must come first. He had provided a home for her, even if not a very loving one, and now it was up to her to take care of him while he needed her.

She felt Craig's hand touch hers and turned her head to see him looking at her anxiously. 'Try not to worry too much,' he encouraged her. 'People who have strokes quite often recover completely.'

Charlotte gave him a forced smile of thanks but didn't believe him, and sat silent again for the rest of the journey.

They went straight to the hospital where they found that Hartford Page was in intensive care and still unconscious. 'I'm sorry,' the doctor on duty told them, 'I have absolutely no idea when he might come round. Or even,' he added firmly but kindly, 'whether he'll come round at all.'

There was nothing they could do, so Craig persuaded Charlotte to go home for the rest of the night. She went reluctantly, feeling that she ought to stay, and already feeling guilty for having gone to London and left her father.

Renate was waiting up for her, and made no comment when she saw that Charlotte had a man with her. The housekeeper led the way into the big old kitchen and they sat round the table drinking coffee while she told them what had happened.

'I was busy preparing dinner,' she said in a flat, unemotional tone. 'Your father was up in his study as always, and when he didn't come down at seven I decided to take a tray up for him. He was lying on the floor. His typewriter was on top of him, and lots of sheets of paper. I suppose he must have held on to the typewriter when he fell.' She raised her eyes to Charlotte's and then reached out her hand to clasp hers tightly, oh, so tightly.

Craig stood up and said, 'Excuse me,' quietly and went out of the room, leaving them alone.

'They said at the hospital,' Renate said stiltedly, taking care over her English, 'that it is very serious. To be prepared, because he may die.'

'Yes, they told me that too.' Charlotte held the older woman's hand, looking into her stricken face, only now realising what had kept Renate loyal to the soul-destroying task of looking after her father and the Abbey for so long.

They didn't say anything else, it wasn't necessary, and when Craig came back ten minutes or so later he found them sitting quietly finishing their coffee.

Charlotte stirred when he came in and said abstractedly, 'I suppose there are things I ought to do.' She said goodnight to Renate and went into the sitting-room with Craig. 'Would—would you like to stay tonight?' She said it tentatively, remembering with fierce regret what they had planned, and unsure now what he would expect of her.

'I think that might be a good idea. Perhaps we could make a bed up in one of the spare rooms?'

Charlotte nodded with a sense of relief. She would have liked to spend the night close in his arms, to have him comfort her and hold her, but now wasn't the time for lovemaking, and they were too attracted physically to be able to spend a night together for the first time without wanting to be closer still. Charlotte realised this and accepted it. But at least Craig would be close and would support her all he could.

She held out her hand to him and he took it and drew her to him, held her in his embrace, his face in her hair, for a long moment. But then he said softly, 'Charlie, there's one thing you must do.'

'What's that?' She lifted tired eyes to look at him.

Craig hesitated briefly, then he said, 'You have to let Verity know what's happened. You must tell her to come home.'

Instinctively she recoiled from the thought, her whole body growing tense, but she realised that he was right almost at once, and slowly nodded. 'Yes, all right, I'll call her. Her phone number is in Daddy's study.'

'Would you like me to do it for you?' Craig offered.

'No!' She said it far too sharply, then bit her lip and shook her head. 'Sorry. No, I'll do it.' And she turned on reluctant feet to summons the sister she had only that day shut out of her mind.

Craig stayed at the Abbey for the next couple of days and offered to stay on longer. Charlotte had made him up a bed in one of the guest rooms and he slept in it for what little was left of that first night, and took her to the hospital again the next day. But all they did was sit and wait in helpless frustration, so on the Monday she said to him, 'Look, I appreciate your offering to stay, but there's really nothing you can do. Renate and I can take it in turns to go to the hospital.'

Craig's eyes narrowed into a frown. 'Are you saying I'm in the way here?'

'No—no, of course not. But it seems so unfair for you to have all this shoved on to you, when we're not even... We didn't even...' She stopped, her cheeks colouring.

Putting his hand on her neck, Craig slowly ran his thumb down the column of her throat. 'Idiot! You know how much I care about you. And I should like to stay here if I can help in even the smallest way. Even if it's only running you to and from the hospital. And if you need me for anything else, I'll be around. OK?'

She nodded gratefully and he leant forward to kiss her before he let her go. But then he spoiled everything by asking what Verity had said when Charlotte had phoned. She told him and he frowned. 'She ought to come,' he said shortly. 'Perhaps it might help if I talked to her and explained just how ill your father is.'

'But I've already told her,' Charlotte protested. 'I've begged and pleaded with her to come, but she won't leave the film she's working on.'

'Perhaps she's under contract to finish it,' Craig suggested. He put a hand over hers. 'Don't worry about it, darling.'

But the very fact that he had mentioned Verity again worried her. Was he thinking about her, wondering what she was like now, if she'd changed much in the six years she'd been away? Was he looking forward to meeting her again, even though they'd parted on such bad terms? Charlotte tried to push the thoughts aside, but there hadn't been enough time since he'd told her his feelings about Verity for her to be absolutely convinced that he was no longer interested. By not trusting him, Charlotte knew that she was denigrating her own power to attract him, but she had lost out so often to Verity in the past, and her love for Craig was so deep, and therefore vulnerable, that she was terrified that everything would change when her sister came home.

She tried desperately to overcome her fears and hoped that Craig would just think she was worried about her father. Fiercely she told herself she was doing him an injustice, and it was just her own stupid jealousy, but it was like a festering sore that wouldn't heal.

Bitter lines drew down Charlotte's mouth as she thought of her father lying in hospital, dying for want of Verity. And of Craig, the man she loved—was he too looking forward to Verity's return? Both the men in her life, turning their backs on her in favour of her sister.

Craig left a couple of days later because he had to get back to work, but he rang every day, saying words of encouragement, asking after her father, of course, but always asking about Verity too. Because of this, Charlotte's manner towards him became almost abrupt, the prejudice overcoming her aching need for him. She longed to tell him she loved him and that she missed him dreadfully, but somehow the words wouldn't come and she was short with him instead. She could tell by his strained voice that he felt it, and she tried not to be like that, but she just couldn't help it.

Hartford Page clung to life for nearly two weeks, and then died in the coma from which he had shown no real signs of emerging. Charlotte spent most of that time by his side, holding his hand, talking to him continuously, trying to pull him back into consciousness. Once, when she went to the hospital one morning, Charlotte took his hand and he seemed to grip hers and to turn his head towards her. Eagerly she began to talk to him, but as soon as she spoke his grip relaxed and he was as deeply unconscious as before. He thought I was Verity—the intituitive thought came into her mind so firmly that Charlotte was quite sure it was true. If it had been Verity, he would have come round, but even to save his life he wouldn't bother for me.

Although Verity was the last person Charlotte wanted to see in England, she rang her again and begged her to come home, convinced that only her presence could save her father's life. But Verity had explained that she was committed to a part in a film and couldn't possibly leave the States at the moment. She would come as soon as she could, she assured Charlotte. Probably in a week or so.

'Surely you could come, even if it's only for a day?' Charlotte found herself begging. 'I'm sure your being here would be good for him. It might even bring him out of the coma.'

'I just can't,' Verity answered irritably. 'I've told you; we're working to a very tight shooting schedule and I just can't let the film company down.'

Angry now, Charlotte said sharply, 'If you don't come, he may die. Don't you care? He cared enough for you.'

'You're being childish,' Verity returned just as sharply. 'If you can't cope, leave things to Renate. And I'm sure you're exaggerating about my making any difference to his condition. Look, I'll call you every day and you can let me know how he is. I'm sure he'll soon recover.'

So his beloved elder daughter didn't come, and Hartford Page eventually gave up and died.

It was in the early hours of Thursday morning, when he was alone. It was almost as though if he couldn't have Verity he wanted no one, defying his younger daughter who had spent so many patient hours at his side. The hospital telephoned the news and Charlotte went up to her father's study, a place that had always been banned to her. She sat down in his chair, looking about her at the shelves piled with books, at the desk where he had spent so many hours, in his youth and middle age in happy creativity, but in his last years in such bitter frustration. Charlotte sat in the room for a long time, remembering the past and trying to think of the happy times. On the desk, placed so that he could see it easily, was a silver-framed photograph of Verity. It was a posed publicity photo, taken when she had just left drama school and was about to launch herself into the acting profession. Hair and make-up were perfect, and she looked very beautiful. She was smiling happily, fully aware of her own beauty—quite confident that it would take her wherever she wanted to go. Now her eyes seemed to be looking at Charlotte tauntingly, and in a sudden moment of inferiority, Charlotte had no doubts whatsoever that Verity could take Craig from her any time she wanted to.

There were no other photographs on the desk. Charlotte heard Renate moving around in the kitchen and went down to tell her the news, then put on a jacket and went for a long walk over the hills.

Craig came down again as soon as she rang and told him, and was very helpful with the arrangements for the funeral. Verity rang very late that night and Charlotte stood up to answer the phone, half expecting Craig to take it for her, but he didn't, and even that made her feel a little better as she abruptly told Verity that their father had died and the date of the funeral. She listened while the other girl spoke, then replaced the phone and turned to Craig. 'She's going to move heaven and earth to make the funeral,' she said bitterly. 'She thinks she should be able to fly over the day before and she wants to be met at the airport. It seems she doesn't feel confident of driving over here after driving on the wrong side of the road for so long.'

'Seems reasonable,' Craig remarked, his eyes on her face.

Charlotte glanced at him and then looked away, knowing that ordinarily he would have offered to meet Verity and bring her down. But he wasn't offering, so did that mean he had realised she was still jealous? Or was he waiting for her to show that she trusted him? Charlotte knew then what she must do, but it was very hard. Trying to still the fear, she lifted her chin and said, 'I expect Renate and I will be busy preparing the food for the funeral the day before; so do you think you might be able to meet Verity? If you can't, of course, I'll...'

But Craig stood up and came across to her, a warm light in his eyes. 'I'll do it.' Putting his arms round her, he held her for a long moment, and Charlotte was infinitely glad that she'd done the right thing. 'Come on,' he said. 'You've had a hell of a day. It's time I tucked you up in bed.'

And he did too, coming into her room when she was in bed and lying down on top of the covers beside her to kiss her goodnight, then holding her until she fell asleep in his arms, all her fears at peace.

But the next morning, over breakfast, when they were working out what other arrangements they had to make for the funeral, Charlotte said, 'I'm surprised Verity's going to come at all.'

'Good heavens, why?' Craig asked in surprise.

'She hates funerals.'

'She would hardly miss her own father's.'

'Why not? She didn't go to Mother's.'

'She was only a child then,' Craig said with indulgent reproof.

Not such a child, Charlotte thought. Verity had been sixteen, old enough to know what was expected of her. But she had locked herself in her room, refusing point blank to go, and of course their father hadn't insisted, although he would have liked her support. He had told everyone that Verity was overcome by grief, and in the end had come to believe it himself.

Her face must have mirrored her thoughts, because she glanced up and caught Craig watching her with a slight frown. Charlotte swallowed and made a supreme effort, managing a small smile. 'I'm sorry—it's just that there are so many things to think about. I expect—once the funeral's over...'

'Yes, of course.' His hand gripped hers. 'And then we'll be able to think of ourselves.'

She nodded, devoutly wishing the same, and hoping he would go on, but he didn't, and she got up to make some fresh coffee. She brought it over and, when she was sitting down again, said, 'You're due to ride in a couple of races tomorrow, aren't you?'

'Yes, but of course I'll cancel them.'

'No, you mustn't do that!' Charlotte was truly horrified. 'You can't let the owners and trainers down at the last minute.'

'I'm sure when I explain the circumstances...'

'No!' Charlotte shook her head determinedly. 'You must ride. Otherwise they might not offer you any more races.' She held up her hand before he could interrupt. 'I really appreciate it, Craig, but I shall be perfectly all right with Renate. We intend to—to go through some of Father's things and take them to Oxfam. There'll be lots to do and I shall be busy, so please don't worry about me.'

Eventually she persuaded him and he left later that evening, but when Charlotte got up the next morning she found Renate too packed and ready to leave. There was no need to ask why, but Charlotte still asked her to stay. 'I need you too, you know,' she said pleadingly, remembering how she had always gone to Renate as she would to a mother, because her own had died when she was only ten.

But Renate shook her head determinedly. 'No, I will leave today.'

'But where will you go? What will you do?' Charlotte asked helplessly. 'This has been your home for fourteen years.'

'I shall go back to Germany. My sister is a widow and I will live with her. It will be good to be home again.'

Charlotte studied her sadly, wishing she had taken the trouble to get to know Renate better, but she had always been there, part of the background, and Charlotte had grown up taking her presence for granted. 'Won't you even stay for the funeral? You're part of our family, you know.'

Renate gave a thin smile. 'No, I will go home. I have sent for a taxi.'

Hurt, Charlotte said, 'That wasn't necessary. You know I would have taken you wherever you want to go.'

Putting out her work-worn hand to touch Charlotte's for a moment, Renate said, 'You were always a nice child. I always hoped that one day he would come to need me, but he never did, not even when he took me to...' She broke off abruptly and stood up. 'But it was always Verity, he had no room in his heart for anyone else. But she never really cared about him, it was all pretence. I don't wish to stay here and see her again.'

The car came soon after and the two women embraced awkwardly, both knowing that they would never see one another again. And so Charlotte was left to go through her father's things and to prepare for the funeral alone.

Craig rang every day, but she didn't tell him about Renate, and she didn't see him again until the evening before the funeral when he brought Verity to the Abbey.

Charlotte knew that they were coming and had got the rooms ready. When they arrived she happened to be in her bedroom and looked out of her window. Immediately she was carried back to the day six years ago when she had looked out of the same window and seen Craig for the first time. And had fallen instantly in love with him. But in what different circumstances! She watched as he helped her sister out of the car. Verity looked up at the house and said something that made them both laugh, and Craig put a familiar hand under her arm as they walked up the stone steps and through the open door.

Verity was lovelier than ever. She still looked twenty instead of twenty-eight, and was even thinner than when she'd left England. There was a manicured sleekness to her now, a sophistication that had only been a veneer before but now was perfectly natural. They were in the drawing-room. Verity was smiling up at Craig, her face animated and sparkling. Craig too looked amused and happy. When they heard Charlotte come in, they turned, and Verity's face immediately became coldly critical. Beside her, Charlotte felt dull and dowdy, and jealousy made her say sharply, 'So you made it at last?'

'Charlie, darling!' Verity came over and kissed her. 'You poor thing! I'm so sorry you've had to go through all this on your own. I came as soon as I could. And now that I'm here you won't have to worry about a thing.' She turned to smile at Craig and held her hand out to him. 'And I know that Craig will help us.'

'Of course.' He took her hand and smiled at her. 'I've already told Charlie that I'll do anything I can.' Letting go of Verity's hand, he came over to Charlotte and kissed her. 'Hello, darling. How are you?'

'How strange that you two should get together!'

There was a note of amused amazement in Verity's tone which Charlotte caught at once, but Craig didn't seem to notice. Ignoring it, Charlotte smiled and said, 'I'm fine.' Then she turned to her sister. 'I expect you're tired after your journey. I got your old room ready for you, if you'd like to go up.'

'In a moment. I'd better go and say hello to Renate first.'

She moved to go to the kitchen, but Charlotte said, 'She isn't here any more. She's gone back to Germany.'

Verity turned to stare at her. 'You fired her? How could you? We need her.'

'No, of course not. She wanted to leave. I couldn't stop her.'

'You could at least have made her stay until I got here to deal with it,' Verity said impatiently. She sighed. 'Still, I suppose you did your best. We'll just have to cope without her.'

'When did she go?' Craig asked.

'Last Saturday. She was all packed and ready to leave when I got up. She—she had nothing to stop for, you see.'

Craig nodded, but said, 'You shouldn't have been here on your own. Why didn't you tell me when I rang? I would have come down.'

'I know.' She smiled, grateful for his concern. 'That's why I didn't tell you. I was quite all right—really.'

Verity broke in to ask about the funeral arrangements. 'What about the food and everything without Renate to do it?'

'It's all taken care of. There's a young woman in the village who's going to come and help.'

'Well, I'm glad you've been able to settle that, at least,' Verity said in a resigned voice. 'I think I'd like to change. Perhaps you wouldn't mind taking my cases up to my room for me, Craig darling?'

'Craig darling' obliged, and when he came down again suggested that they all go out to dinner.

'I've already made a casserole,' Charlotte objected.

'It will keep, won't it? Come on, Charlie, it will do you good to get out of the house for a while. You look tired.'

'Oh, thanks a million!'

He laughed and kissed her. 'Go and get ready. It will be much better all round.'

She hesitated for a moment longer and then nodded, knowing he was right. It would be much easier to get through tonight in a public place rather than trying to make strained conversation at home.

Craig booked a table in a restaurant in a nearby village that was popular with tourists and summer visitors, and they saw no one they knew. If he felt any embarrassment at being with his ex- and his current girlfriend, he certainly didn't show it, handling the situation with his usual assertive self-confidence. Verity did most of the talking—naturally; telling them all about her life and acting career in America, raising her voice loud enough for the people at the nearest tables to be in no doubt that they had a celebrity in their midst. She asked a couple of perfunctory questions about Charlotte's job, but was much more interested in Craig's, asking him among other things whether he had converted any old houses into flats. If Charlotte had been her normal self she might have picked that up and taken warning from it, but she was too tense to notice. All her anxious attention was on Craig, wondering if he was again falling under Verity's spell. She watched his face, trying to see how he was reacting to her sister's flattery, listened to his voice to catch any trace of emotion or admiration in his tone.

Often Craig glanced up and caught her watching him, and at first smiled encouragingly, even winked at her once, but towards the end of the evening began to have a little frown in his eyes. He tried to draw her into the conversation, but Verity soon shut her out again. Not that Charlotte tried very hard anyway; she felt like an outsider, an unwanted chaperon.

When they finished their coffee Craig stood up and said decisively, 'If you'll excuse me, I'll go and pay the bill.'

Verity's pink-painted mouth pouted disappointedly. 'Going already?'

'You girls have a long day ahead of you tomorrow.'

'Yes, and I am starting to feel a little jet-lagged. So sweet of you to think of me, Craig darling.' He went away and she turned to Charlotte. 'How long have you been going out with him?'

'Only a few months.'

'I'm surprised. I shouldn't have thought you were his type,' Verity commented, watching Craig as he paid the bill.

'Maybe he went off your type,' Charlotte surprised herself by retorting acidly.

Verity looked amused. 'Oh, don't worry, darling, I've got much bigger fish on my hook. You're welcome to him.' A reminiscent look came into her eyes. 'He was fun, though.'

Craig drove them home and they all went upstairs together, an amused look coming into Verity's face as she saw the two of them go to different rooms. Hell, let her laugh, Charlotte thought fiercely as she shut her door, I couldn't care less. But she did care, desperately. And she needed Craig so much. If Verity hadn't been there, she knew she would have run to his room. But it was because Verity was there that she so urgently wanted the reassurance of his closeness. How much longer would her sister stay? she wondered. She couldn't be expected to leave on the day of the funeral, of course, but maybe she would go the day after, so that she could be happy with Craig again.

Charlotte lay in bed, forcing herself to think of what it would be like when Verity was out of their lives again, but it wasn't easy; she had lost out too many times to Verity to have any confidence in her own powers to hold Craig. All she could do was to pray that Verity would hurry up and go. Sleep didn't come that night, and it showed when she dressed for the funeral the next morning. She had done everything herself, made all the preparations, but it was Verity who took over as grieving hostess the moment the first guest arrived. Dressed entirely in black and looking very fragile and lovely, her sister managed to give the impression of barely held-back grief as she greeted the guests, and soon had them commiserating with her because she hadn't been able to get back in time to see her father alive. 'The entire studio,' Charlotte heard her murmur in a suitably tragic voice, 'depending on me. Couldn't let them down. Had to try to hide my heartbreak.'

Craig was a tower of strength, standing between Verity and Charlotte at the funeral and letting Charlotte hold his hand tightly. And afterwards he opened car doors, handed round drinks and generally acted as host. Charlotte was grateful, but caught several people looking at him, wondering which sister he was with. It seemed to go on for ever, first the funeral service in the local parish church, then the long, slow ride to the crematorium and another service there, then the reception at the Abbey afterwards.

But at last they all left. Charlotte hadn't expected there to be so many people, but quite a few villagers had come along, as well as some of Hartford Page's friends and a representative from his publishers. It was the villagers, who lived nearest, who were the last to go, and it wasn't until the evening that Verity could switch off her act and drop into an armchair. 'God, I'm exhausted. Get me a good stiff drink, Craig. Couldn't you have given them a hint to leave earlier, Charlie?'

'They were much too fascinated listening to the local filmstar,' Charlotte returned shortly, and was surprised to see Craig grin.

'Well, I'm hungry, and I'm sure Craig is, too. How long will dinner be?'

'I've already put yesterday's casserole in the oven. It shouldn't take long.'

'Yesterday's casserole!' Verity turned up her delicate nose. 'Come back, Renate, all is forgiven. Still, I suppose it will have to do. I'm going upstairs; call me when it's ready.'

Following Charlotte into the kitchen, Craig put a hand on her shoulder. 'Don't let her get you down.'

She turned to him quickly, eagerly, and he took her in his arms and gently stroked her back. 'I don't know why she came,' Charlotte mumbled against his chest. 'She hasn't shown any feelings at all, not real feelings. Everything today—even when she cried—it was all for effect.'

'I know. But you must remember that Verity hadn't seen your father for several years. And maybe she feels grief differently from you. Maybe she's just bottled it all away—that's the worst kind.'

So he was defending Verity now. Charlotte gave a tight smile and drew away. 'I'd better get dinner.'

They called Verity and she came down, holding a long envelope. 'I've found a copy of Daddy's will,' she told them triumphantly. Sitting down at the table, she opened it there and then and began to go quickly through it.

'Do you have to do that now?' Charlotte demanded, pain raw in her voice. 'Can't you wait till tomorrow?'

'A lot of things might depend on it,' Verity pointed out, still reading. 'Yes, it's much as I expected. He's left everything to be divided equally between us. He always did fall over backwards to be fair to you.'

'Did he—did he leave anything to Renate?' Charlotte couldn't resist asking.

Verity looked at her in surprise. 'To Renate? No, why should he?' She turned to Craig. 'Darling, I have a proposition to put to you.' Then she gave a tinkling laugh. 'No, darling, don't look so eager, it isn't *that* kind of proposition!' Her face became intent and somehow sharper. 'I've been thinking about this house, and I think the only thing we can do is to turn it into apartments and sell them off. Perhaps even sell them as time-share apartments. That would make more money but would probably take more time to sell, of course. What do you think as an architect; would it be possible to convert the house?'

Craig shrugged. 'Everything's possible, of course. But what does Charlie think of the idea?'

'I don't want it broken up,' Charlotte answered instantly. 'This is my home. I want to go on living here.'

'Well, there's your answer,' Craig remarked.

'Really? Not quite so fast!' Verity leaned forward. 'Can you afford to pay for the upkeep of this house, Charlie? And what's even more important, can you afford to buy out my share—on your own?' She looked from one to the other of them. 'I take it you are on your own?'

'Yes, I'm on my own,' Charlotte said into the unendurable silence that followed. 'And there's no way I can give you a cash payment if you demand your half now.

But when—if—you come back to England, you'll want somewhere to live and...'

'But I may never come back, and even if I did I certainly wouldn't want to live in this godforsaken place. Look, Charlie, you haven't bothered to think. If we turn this house into flats you could have one for yourself. That way you could go on living here without the worry of keeping it going. *And* you'd have quite a nice little nest-egg besides.'

Charlotte pushed her plate away, her face white and taut. 'Do you have to talk about this now? Today of all days? How can you?'

'I can talk about it because I haven't got time for sentimentality. Oh, for heaven's sake, Charlie! What difference is it going to make whether we discuss it today or tomorrow? There's a lot to do, and I want it all signed and settled before I go back to the States.' She turned to Craig. 'Now, darling, would you be willing to take over as architect of the project?'

'If Charlie doesn't want to do it...'

'Charlie doesn't have any choice,' Verity cut in. 'One way or another the Abbey has got to be sold, and sold immediately, because I want my share now. So if we're going to sell it I don't see why we can't make as much profit as possible out of it. Do you?'

Craig glanced at Charlotte, but she sat silently, her face grim, her hands held tightly in her lap. 'It isn't as simple as that,' he pointed out. 'Converting the house into flats would cost a great deal of money. Where are you going to raise the capital to do it?'

'I can get some. But I don't know if...'

'I thought you said you were hard up,' Charlotte broke in. 'That you wanted your share of the house now? You just said that to try and force my hand.'

'This is an investment,' Verity pointed out coldly. 'And that's why I want my share of this house—to invest it. I certainly don't intend to forgo my share just so that you can go on mooning around here the rest of your life.' Again she gave her attention to Craig. 'How much do you think it will cost?'

'It's difficult to say without drawing up detailed plans and working out an estimate.'

'Would you do that for me—tomorrow?' wheedled Verity, giving him one of her famous smiles. 'I'd be most terribly grateful if you would, darling.'

'It's hardly something that can be done in a day.'

'Not in precise detail, no. But surely you could give me an idea of how much it would cost?'

'Possibly. But only if Charlie agrees.'

'Oh, don't mind me,' Charlotte said bitterly. 'Just go ahead and do what you want.' Getting up, she took her still full plate out to the kitchen, washed it up, then went through the kitchen door out into the overgrown garden that had once been her mother's pride and pleasure.

It was still light, although the shadows were very long now. Leaning against the garden wall, she looked back at the house. Was she to lose that as well as everything else? And Craig? He had taken Verity's side with only the smallest hesitation. But what could she do about it? She had little money of her own, most of her salary having gone into maintaining the house and paying Renate. Not that Verity had bothered to take that into account, of course.

She turned and looked away from the house. Maybe she was a fool to want to stay here. Maybe it would be better to make a clean break. She certainly didn't want to stay on here when the house was full of other people using rooms that she thought of as hers or her father's. Planting their own gardens. Especially when they would know who she was. They would probably be sympathetic towards her, ask her the history of the place, or regard her as a glorified caretaker and push all their complaints on to her. Charlotte gave a mental shudder and decided anything was better than that.

Think positively, she told herself. You can't afford to go on living here, so be like Verity; make as much as you can out of it and let it go, memories and all. Her mind went back to the dinner-table, when Verity had asked if she was alone and Craig had remained silent. But what could he have said? He liked her, he had taken her out, he had almost gone to bed with her. And he had been very supportive since her father's illness. What more could she ask? But Charlotte would have given anything for him to have stretched out his hand to take hers and said, 'No, Charlie isn't alone.'

Wandering through the garden, Charlotte came to the paddock, where she kicked off her shoes and sat on the fence to watch the horses. They both came up to her, whickering gently, and Charlotte stroked their noses, first one and then the other. 'No, I'm sorry, I haven't got anything for you tonight. Not even a carrot.'

Footsteps sounded on the ground, but she didn't turn round as Craig came up to lean against the fence beside her.

'How does the mare ride?' he asked.

For a while they talked horses, but Charlotte knew it was only a preamble and he had something else on his mind. It hardly took a genius to guess what, and her mouth twisted cynically when, after a short silence, Craig said, 'Have you thought any more about Verity's idea?'

'Her proposition? What choice do I have? I doubt very much if any bank or building society would lend me the money to buy her half. And even if one did, there are such a lot of repairs that need to be done, as well as the ordinary household bills. I could never manage it all on my own.' An idea came to her and she said thoughtfully, 'Maybe I could let part of it, though. Or do bed and breakfast for summer visitors.'

'Wouldn't that be much the same as turning it into flats? You'd still have lots of strangers living here, but with far less profit and with a great deal more work and worry yourself. Does the Abbey really mean that much to you?'

'Whose side are you on, Craig?'

'I just want what's best for you, Charlie.'

Her voice bitter, Charlotte said, 'Did Verity send you out here to try to persuade me?' He was silent and she said, 'I *thought* so. Did you always do her bidding? Verity never does anything unpleasant herself.'

'She asked me to speak to you, yes. But I was going to talk to you about it anyway. She wants me to draw up conversion plans, but I won't if you don't want me to.'

'If I say no, she'll only get someone else.'

'Yes, I expect so. But even so, she can't legally go ahead unless you agree.'

'And if I don't?'

'Then she would probably go to an estate agent to get a valuation on the property, and then to a solicitor who would write to you stipulating a date by which you would have to pay Verity her share of the value or put the house up for sale.'

'And if I can't meet it?'

'Then she would be entitled to go over your head and sell the house.'

'And have me evicted if I refused to leave, I suppose?' Craig nodded silently and she said bitterly, 'I was right, then; I don't have any choice.'

'Actually it isn't a bad idea, Charlie. And at least you would know that the house was still standing and being lived in, not pulled down for development. And if you wanted a flat here, I'm sure we...'

'You don't have to go on,' she said sharply. 'You've done what you were sent to do. But I don't see why I should just stand by and let her tear the house apart just to make a profit. No, you can go back and tell my beloved sister that I'm going to fight her every step of the way!' Jumping down to put on her shoes, Charlotte caught hold of the mare's mane. 'Well, go on, what are you waiting for? Verity won't like it if you keep *her* waiting, you know!' Grasping the mane, she slid on to the horse's back.

'Don't be so damn silly. Where are you going?' Craig started to climb the fence, but the horse was already backing away.

'Riding, of course.'

'At night? It will soon be dark. Don't be a little fool!'

But Charlotte laughed on a high note of bitter self-mockery and gave the horse its head, ignoring Craig's shout as she disappeared into the gathering darkness.

CHAPTER FIVE

CRAIG was waiting for her when Charlotte got back to the house some time later, his face grim, but it softened when he saw she had been crying.

'My poor darling, you've had a hell of a day, haven't you?'

He put his arm round her and Charlotte leaned her head against his shoulder, grateful for the comfort it gave her. 'I'm sorry,' she murmured. 'The funeral, Verity—it all got a bit too much.'

'I know.' He kissed her on the temple, gently lifting her hair out of the way. 'You look tired to death. Go on up to bed and try not to worry. It will all sort itself out.'

'Will it?' She looked into his face for reassurance, wondering—if her father hadn't been taken ill when he did—whether Craig would have proposed to her that night. Whether she would have been his fiancée now. As it was, she felt in a strange state of limbo, without the right to call on his support against Verity as she could have done if they were engaged, or even if they had become lovers. That, too, would have created a closer bond to their relationship that she could have relied on and it would have given her strength. But now she still felt alone, her relationship with him not much different from what his had been with her sister.

'Of course.' He kissed her again, on the lips this time, but soon raised his head as he insisted again that she go and get some sleep.

Charlotte was glad enough to obey him, but she only slept because she was just too exhausted to stay awake fretting any longer.

But when she awoke in the morning she felt better, bouncing back with the resilience of youth and feeling much more herself again. She lay awake for a while, looking up at the patterns several damp patches had made on the ceiling over the years, and smiled to herself. The house would have to be sold, she'd known that all along; if she couldn't afford to repair the roof, then how on earth could she possibly afford to buy Verity out and maintain it? Last night she had just been silly—no, not silly, upset by Verity's insensitivity. She jumped out of bed, determined to be practical and to keep an open mind about turning the house into flats. Just because the idea came from Verity, it didn't necessarily mean that it was a bad one. And Craig had seemed to think that it might be possible.

She put on jeans and a sweater and went downstairs, but Verity had left her door ajar and was on the watch for her, and when she heard her steps pulled the door wide and said peremptorily, 'Come in here. I want a word with you.'

Charlotte hesitated, thinking about Craig. 'Can't it wait until after breakfast? I . . .'

'No. Now.' Verity stood back and Charlotte walked past her into the bedroom, a room that their father had insisted on keeping ready in case Verity had ever come back home. It was a good large room, with windows on two sides that looked out over the fields and meadows to the distant hills. And here there were no damp patches because Hartford Page had paid for a decorator to come in every spring and repaint it, so that it would always be clean and fresh for his elder daughter. Not that Verity cared—she didn't even have to pretend she cared now.

Charlotte determinedly pushed that thought aside and turned to face her sister. Verity was still undressed, wearing a most beautiful négligé of blue silk and lace that hung full and loose from her shoulders, a dream of a garment that made Charlotte sigh with envy. Verity wasn't wearing make-up either, but she was still young enough to look almost as beautiful without it. For a moment Charlotte again felt the plain sister and said rather sharply, 'What do you want? If it's about the house...'

'You bet your sweet life it is,' Verity retorted. 'Craig told me just what you said last night, and if it's a fight you want, then you're damn well going to get it—and lose!'

'He told you?' Charlotte felt a stab of betrayal.

'Of course.' Verity glared at her angrily. 'Did you think he was on your side?' she sneered. 'Well, he isn't, he agrees with me completely on this. We both think you're being a stupid, stubborn idiot.'

'He didn't say that. He wouldn't,' Charlotte protested, her face pale.

'Oh, for God's sake, Charlie, grow up! Do you really think Craig enjoys having you mooning over him like a lovesick little fool? I can...'

'Shut up! Leave Craig out of this!'

'That will be rather difficult when he's going to draw up the alterations to the house.'

'He hasn't said he will,' Charlotte pointed out angrily, 'and *I* haven't said I'm going to let you go ahead with it.'

'You don't have any choice. I can easily go to law and get you thrown out. And as for Craig——' Verity paused and looked at Charlotte tauntingly '—he'll do just whatever I want him to.'

Charlotte drew in her breath sharply, recognising the challenge that had been thrown at her. 'No,' she said firmly. 'You're wrong—so wrong.'

'Am I?' Verity strode up to her and glared into her face. 'Don't think I've forgotten how you turned Craig against me before.'

'He'd already heard things about you; he told me,' Charlotte returned.

'Those were just spiteful rumors,' Verity dismissed them with a wave of her hand. 'Craig would never have believed them if you hadn't put your spiteful little oar in. Well, now you're going to see how *you* like it. You think he's yours, don't you? But you're going to find out just how wrong you are. I only have to crook my little finger and he'll come running back to me.'

For a moment fear filled Charlotte's heart, but then she remembered how she'd talked of this with Craig and her chin came up. 'He was already tiring of you, he told me so. He said—he said you sickened him.'

'Oh, did he now?' Verity's lovely face sharpened, making her suddenly seem hard and scheming. 'Well, maybe I'll make him pay for that, too. But first I'm going to teach you a lesson you'll never forget.' She looked at Charlotte derisively. 'You—keep a man when I want him? The idea's laughable!'

Charlotte's hands balled into tight fists and she drew herself up to her full height. At least she was taller than her sister, could look down on her and say with dignity, 'I'm in love with Craig, and I know he cares about me.'

Verity pounced swiftly. 'But he hasn't told you that he's in love with you, has he?'

'Well, he certainly wasn't in love with *you*,' Charlotte fired back. 'He told me all about it.'

'Interested, were you?' sneered Verity. 'Couldn't believe your luck, I expect. And just what did he tell you?'

'That you hadn't meant anything to him. That there was nothing serious between you and...' Charlotte broke off as Verity gave a peal of laughter.

'He told you that, did he? My God, you must be unsure of yourself if you had to find out whether we'd been to bed together!' She saw Charlotte's cheeks flare and pushed on with her attack. 'And he told you we hadn't. Well, Craig always was a gentleman, but then he could hardly say anything else, could he?'

'You're lying!' Charlotte retorted, her voice rising. 'He was never your lover.'

Again Verity laughed spitefully. 'How naïve you are, even now. A man tells a woman what she wants to hear. And it's more than obvious that you were dying for a sop to boost your inferior little ego. Of course we were lovers. But Craig just couldn't stand the thought of me with another man. He was so jealous.'

'You admit there were other men, then?'

'No one who mattered. But Craig mattered, and now I'm going to get him back.'

'You're wrong. He doesn't want you.'

'No?' Verity gave her an amused look. 'Just make the most of him, little sister, because you won't have him for much longer.' A reflective look came into her eyes. 'I wonder what he saw in you in the first place—or perhaps he only started dating you because you were my sister.'

'Oh, for God's sake! You're perverted by your own egotism!' And, unable to take any more, Charlotte turned and ran from the room.

She halted for a few moments at the bottom of the stairs, striving to get a hold on her emotions, but she was still shaking with anger when she walked into the kitchen and found Craig there, getting himself some breakfast.

'Good morning.' He gave her a sharp glance. 'I'm doing myself a couple of poached eggs. Want some?'

'N-no, thanks. I don't feel hungry.'

'How are you this morning? Feeling rested?'

'What? Oh, yes, I suppose so.'

Craig poured a cup of coffee and gave it to her. 'Here, drink this, it will make you feel better.' She took it and after a couple of minutes he said, 'So you're still going to fight Verity over the house?'

Her mind had been full of what Verity had said, but now Charlotte lifted her head to look at Craig. 'Why do you say that?'

'Well, the fight's already started, hasn't it? I heard you two yelling at each other when I came downstairs.'

Charlotte flushed, thinking how undignified it had all become. Before, everything had been so perfect, so right.

Now her love for Craig seemed to be totally cheapened and spoilt. 'Did you hear?' she asked in embarrassment.

'Not in so many words, no. I just caught the general tone—it was difficult not to.'

'I'm sorry.'

Craig put two plates of eggs on toast on the table and sat down opposite her. 'Eat up your breakfast,' he ordered.

'I said I didn't want any.'

'But I think you do.' He grinned at her. 'I'm not that bad a cook.'

She smiled reluctantly and began to eat, almost immediately feeling better.

'OK?'

She nodded. 'Yes, thanks. I guess I did need to eat.'

Craig poured more coffee. 'Is it really worth fighting over?' he asked evenly, his eyes on her face.

For a moment she could only think of her quarrel with Verity over him, but then realised what he meant. 'Oh, the house. No, I don't suppose it is, really.'

'But you don't see why Verity should have her own way, is that it?'

'If I agreed with that it would just make me seem unnecessarily stubborn and childish.' She expected him to say something, but he didn't, and there was anger in her eyes as she looked at him. 'You told Verity what I said last night,' she said accusingly.

'Wasn't I supposed to? She wanted to know—insisted on knowing. So I told her. I also told her that I thought you'd said it in the heat of the moment and might well change your mind when you'd rested and had time to think it over. *And* I told her she was an idiot to have brought it up on the day of the funeral.'

'Well, thanks for that at least.' Charlotte got up and started taking the dishes over to the sink.

'*At least*?'

'She talked you round to her way of thinking, didn't she? You said last night you thought it wasn't a bad idea to convert the house.'

'Well, is it?' Craig got to his feet and came over to her. 'The house has to go, Charlie, you know that. There's no way you can cope with a place this size, even if I helped you. No one family would want to buy it; it isn't big enough for a school or hotel, so surely the most sensible solution is to turn it into flats? And to do that you have to either sell it cheaply to a developer, or do the alterations yourself so that you get the profit.'

She stood still and turned to look at him, her body tense. 'You make it all sound so simple, don't you? But all you're really saying is do what Verity wants. Just whose side are you on, Craig?'

He gave an impatient gesture. 'Sides don't come into it. It's just common sense. For heaven's sake, try to look at it objectively and stop making it a personal issue between you and Verity.'

'Why does it have to be what she wants? Why can't you think about what *I* want?'

Craig was about to make an angry retort, but Verity came into the kitchen and smiled when she saw their angry faces. 'Tut, tut! A lovers' tiff? Now what could have caused that, I wonder?'

Charlotte turned away from her amused glance, realising with frustrated anger that arguing with Craig was only playing into Verity's hands. 'Do you want any breakfast?' she asked ungraciously.

'No, thanks. Just orange juice will do. What a lovely day,' Verity remarked, going to the window. 'I'd almost forgotten how lovely an English summer can be.' She was wearing beautifully tailored trousers and a silk blouse, looking casual but very elegant. Deliberately she turned, so that the sun was behind her, turning her hair into a golden halo around her head, and smiled at Craig. 'Let's go for a walk, shall we, darling? I want to hear everything you've been doing while I've been away. And we could discuss the conversion of the house too.'

'Don't draw me into this, Verity,' Craig warned.

'Darling, I don't have to. It's perfectly obvious that you already agree with me.' She paused, giving him an opportunity to correct her, but when he remained silent Verity gave what to Charlotte looked a very catlike smile, and went on, 'I'm afraid I have neither the time nor the money to indulge in sentimentality and nostalgia. If you want to fight me over this, Charlie, then that's your privilege, of course, but it will only postpone the inevitable and waste more money on lawyers' fees. I intend to make the most of my inheritance, even if you don't. I'm quite sure that's what Daddy would have wanted,' she added in a tone that sounded to Charlotte straight out of a second-rate film.

'He loved this house,' Charlotte protested. 'As—as I do.'

'But Daddy's gone—and *you're on your own* in this,' Verity stressed, rubbing salt into the wound. She turned to Craig. 'Darling, why don't you talk to her? Try and make her see sense. I'm sure she'd listen to you.'

'Charlie and I have already discussed it,' Craig said evenly. 'She knows my views as an architect, now it's up to her to make up her own mind.'

Verity's face took on a speculative air that Charlotte couldn't stand. She turned to Craig, but his manner was cold and withdrawn and she realised that he was angry at being drawn into their quarrel. Suddenly Charlotte knew there was only one way open to her if she wanted to keep Craig, and not only keep him but keep his good opinion of her. Her chin high, she turned to her sister and said, 'As a matter of fact I've already made up my mind. I was going to tell you earlier, but you were so eager to jump down my throat that you gave me no opportunity. And if you'd waited instead of bringing it up last night when...'

'All right, all right!' snapped Verity. 'Just leave out the self-righteousness and get on with it. What have you decided?'

Forcing herself to be calm, Charlotte said painfully, 'That I won't stop you converting the house.'

Verity gave a triumphant laugh. 'But how wise of you, little sister. How very wise.' Her mouth twisted mockingly. 'But too late, I'm afraid, to make any difference to that other little matter we spoke about this morning. That still stands.'

Charlotte stared at her speechlessly for a moment, then became aware of Craig watching them and quickly bent to pick up the shopping basket. 'I have to go into the village to get some groceries.' She opened the door leading outside and looked back, hoping Craig would follow. He started to do so, but Verity put a hand on his arm and began to speak to him. He stopped and turned towards her.

Charlotte shut the door a lot harder than she'd intended and ran to her car, driving away from the Abbey with a mind filled with guilty hatred towards the sister she ought to love. And Craig? Towards him she felt both anger and resentment, but all mixed up with love and frustrated yearning. She loved him so much, and was petrified that she might lose him. But that wasn't why she'd given way to Verity, even if her sister chose to think so. She had done so because it made sense and because Craig advised it, and all she wanted now was for the legalities to be over and done with so that Verity would go back to the States and leave them in peace.

Walking round the stalls in the village market and the mundane task of shopping helped to calm her, but when she got back to the Abbey Charlotte found that Verity had already started going round the house with Craig, excitedly discussing how the house could be split most advantageously.

Craig came over and kissed Charlotte, looking intently into her eyes. 'You OK?'

She gave him as bright a smile as she could manage. 'Yes, thank you. I thought we might have a salad for lunch, if that's all right. And I thought we...'

'Yes, that's fine,' Verity interrupted. 'Now, Craig, surely we could get a bathroom into that turret, and a kitchen below it. What do you think?'

'It should be possible. But maybe Charlie has some ideas,' he said deliberately, and turned to look at her.

'Of course she hasn't, she isn't interested.' Verity stopped, and looked at her younger sister. 'Have you any ideas?'

'No,' Charlotte said after a moment. 'Do what you like.'

'There, I told you.' Verity was still talking as she went out of the room, but Craig gave Charlotte an almost impatient look before he followed her.

Later, when they were alone in the kitchen, he said abruptly, 'I didn't know you were a poor loser, Charlie.'

'I suppose you're going to tell me why you think I am,' Charlotte answered, her face tightening.

'You've agreed that you have no other choice but to fall in with Verity's ideas. So can't you now at least take an active interest? I'm sure you would have a great deal to contribute. And you know this house better than either of us.'

'Oh, I think I've already made my contribution; I don't see why I should pretend to like the arrangement. And anyway, Verity knows the house as well as I do, so you don't really need me at all.'

'Yes, I do,' Craig said firmly, putting his arms around her. '*I* really need you.' And he bent to take her lips in a lingering kiss.

Charlotte sighed and leant her head against his shoulder. 'Oh, Craig! If only...' She bit her lip and sighed again.

'They're a waste of time, aren't they—if onlys? Regrets have to be pushed out of your mind and you have to get on with the here and now.'

'And I suppose Verity and her ideas are the here and now?'

'I'm afraid so.'

Slowly she said, 'Your—affair with Verity, how long did it last?'

He gave her a quick glance. 'Not all that long. And it wasn't an affair.'

'But it was—was pretty hot while it lasted, wasn't it?'

Craig laughed, 'What a question!' He gave her a sudden sharp look. 'Good God, you're not still jealous of Verity, are you?'

Charlotte's hands balled into tight fists at her sides. 'Should I be?'

'Good heavens, no! You know it was all over years ago. I've already told you that.'

'She's still—beautiful. Perhaps even more so.'

'Possibly. I hadn't noticed.' Putting his hands on her waist, he said, 'What is this, Charlie? You don't seriously think that I'm still attracted to her, do you?'

'You could be, quite easily.'

'Well, I'm not. I suppose I ought to be flattered that you're jealous, but I'm not that either. Surely you know I don't want anyone else?'

She bit her lip and then went into his arms. 'Yes, I do really. I'm sorry—I'm just so tense and nervous at the moment.' But, although Charlotte made the excuse, her heart told her that this wasn't just any woman, this was Verity. And Verity had always got what she wanted, no matter who got hurt.

Charlotte had intended to make up a picnic so that she and Craig could drive to the coast or some place where they could be alone, but Verity raised all sorts of objections and in the end they all finished up eating together off the kitchen table.

'You know my time is limited,' Verity complained. 'If Craig and I can get the basic alterations worked out this weekend he'll probably be able to do the drawings next week. Won't you, darling?' She smiled at Craig. 'It's so wonderful having you to help. I don't know what I'd do without you.'

'I'm quite sure you would have found someone else,' Craig returned evenly. His mouth twisted wryly. 'Only if you'd got some other architect you would obviously have had to pay him the full fee.'

Verity smiled into his eyes. 'Does that mean you're going to do it for old times' sake, darling—or is it for love?' she added, her smile becoming provocative.

A faintly mocking look came into Craig's brown eyes, but then he turned from Verity to Charlotte and said, 'For both, of course.'

In the evening Craig sat at the dining-room table and did some preliminary drawings on sheets of paper taken from the reams of untouched typing paper in the study, and Charlotte, almost reluctantly, went to sit quietly beside him, fascinated by his skill. He smiled at her and started to describe what he was doing, and Charlotte found herself becoming more interested and even making one or two suggestions, which he accepted warmly.

For a little while she began to feel happier, but after an hour or so Verity switched off the television set, came over and said mockingly, 'So you've won Charlie over. Oh, the power of male attraction! Well, have you reached a provisional figure for the alterations yet?'

'I think you'd have to do it in two stages,' Craig replied. 'The main house first and then the two wings.' He sat back in his chair. 'I think the conversion of the main house would cost at least a quarter of a million, maybe more. The whole thing double that.'

Verity's face tightened, and Charlotte felt a stupid surge of hope as she said, 'I can't spare that much to invest. Can't it be done for less?'

'Not if you want to sell the flats at a good price. But you could do the main house first and use the money you get from those flats to finance the rest of the development. That way you'd only have to raise two hundred and fifty thousand to start.'

'It's still too steep. And it would probably be difficult for me to borrow money in England when I've been out of the country for so long.'

Verity looked at Charlotte speculatively, but before she could make the suggestion that was obviously in her mind Craig said smoothly, 'As I seem to be investing my professional services, I might as well invest some money too.'

'Darling, that's wonderful!' Verity's eyes lit and she put a familiar hand on Craig's shoulder. 'How marvellous of you to help me like this.' She gave him a dazzling smile and said eagerly, 'And it will give you even more reason to take an interest in the conversion. How soon do you think we can start?'

'We'll have to get planning permission first, but it shouldn't take too long. Most councils are only too pleased to see historic houses preserved in this way.'

'Excuse me,' Charlotte said abruptly, 'I'm going to bed.' And she got up and walked out of the room.

Behind her she heard Craig's chair scrape, but Verity said, 'Oh, let her go and sulk. How much can you put up?'

So he didn't follow her, and Charlotte went to bed and fell asleep quite quickly, considering. But then she hadn't had a great deal of sleep lately, one way or another.

But she hadn't been in bed for more than an hour when there was a soft rap on the door and Craig came into the room. Switching on her bedside-lamp, Charlotte sat up sleepily, then blushed, her senses beginning to flutter in anticipation. But almost immediately Craig said, 'It's all right, I just want to talk to you.' And her heart sank in disappointment.

Sitting on the edge of the bed, he said, 'Sorry to wake you. I didn't think you'd be asleep yet.'

'What do you want?' Charlotte asked tonelessly.

'Only to explain why I've decided to help out with the financial side of the renovation.'

'You don't have to explain. What you do with your money is your affair. If you want to help Verity...'

'I didn't do it to help Verity,' Craig cut in impatiently, 'I did it to help you.'

'Me?' Charlotte raised her eyebrows. 'I really don't see...'

'No, because you seem to have a blind spot over this. Don't you understand? If I put money into converting the house it will give us more say in how the alterations are done. And it will help to stop Verity getting all her own way, or taking short cuts to save money. I don't want my name associated with shoddy workmanship and sub-standard materials.'

Leaning back against the brass rails of her old bed, Charlotte wondered if this was really why he had done it. Wondered if Craig even understood his own motivation. Was it for practical reasons? Or did he subconsciously feel the need to be near Verity again, even though he hadn't admitted it to himself? Or was it, as he'd said, to help *her*? She frowned. 'I still don't see how it helps me?'

'Because things will go far more smoothly. There'll be a lot less hassle for you to put up with.' Reaching out a hand, he gently stroked her cheek. 'Don't look so worried, my darling. It will work out for the best, believe me. Surely you'd realised that you couldn't go on living here for ever? Hadn't you ever thought about what you would do if your father died?'

'He was so young,' Charlotte answered. 'Not even seventy.'

She looked very young herself as she said it, her face without make-up, her red-gold hair loose on her shoulders, and her eyes wide and vulnerable, smudged with grief and tiredness. Her white cotton nightshirt, which buttoned all down the front, lay open for the first few inches, revealing the top of the valley between her breasts. Unable to resist a surge of desire, Craig undid two more buttons and slid his hand inside. 'Do you remember that night when we first met?' he asked, his voice thickening.

'Yes, I remember.' Her eyes were fixed on his, her lips parting in awareness as he caressed her.

'You look as young and vulnerable tonight as you did then. You make me want to protect you.'

'Pro-protect me? Who from?'

'From the big bad world. From Verity.' Deliberately he pushed her nightshirt aside to reveal her breasts, then bent to kiss them. Charlotte gasped and lifted her arms to grasp the bed rail by her head, her body squirming deliciously.

'I don't—I don't need to be protected,' she answered on a hoarse note of rising eroticism.

'Don't you?' Craig lifted his head, his eyes dark with the nakedness of his need for her. His hand slid down to her waist beneath the bedclothes, but then his jaw hardened and he stood up abruptly. 'Goodnight, Charlie. I'm sorry; I should have let you go on sleeping.' He let himself out of the room, but before he closed the door Charlotte heard Verity's voice as she passed to go to her own room. 'Good heavens, darling, leaving already? You must be losing your touch. Or is my little sister playing hard to get? She doesn't know what she's missing!'

Craig's reply was lost as he firmly closed the thick old door that shut out every sound, but Charlotte could imagine Verity accosting him in the corridor, smiling provocatively up at him in that sexy way she had. Almost, she got out of bed and ran to the door, but something held her back. Pride and the fear of Verity's mockery, probably.

It rained the whole of the next day, so there was no question of going for a picnic. Verity spent most of the day on the phone ringing round old friends, while Craig helped Charlotte to sort through her father's books and put them in bundles ready to send to auction.

'I suppose there's quite a lot of furniture that could go, too,' she said, trying to be constructive.

'That's a good idea.' Verity had come to stand in the doorway, looking sleek and lovely in black velvet trousers and a figured blouse. 'Charlie can put her share of the proceeds into developing the house.'

Craig looked at Charlotte, but when she didn't speak said, 'What Charlie does with her inheritance is her affair. Allowing her half of the house to be used is involvement enough.'

'Well, she needn't expect to get as much back out of the profits as me—or you, for that matter. If she...'

Charlotte stood up angrily. 'Would you mind not talking about me as if I wasn't here? I'll go and get some lunch.'

'Don't bother for me. I've been invited out to lunch— someone from the local newspaper wants to do a feature on me.' Verity turned to Craig. 'I expect you'll be going back to London tonight, won't you?' And when he nodded, she said, 'Oh, good, I'll be able to cadge a lift from you. My agent has booked me to appear on a television chat show tomorrow evening, so I'll stay up in town tonight.'

Verity's lunch date came to pick her up an hour later and Charlotte watched her go. Craig came up behind her as she looked out of the window, and he put his hands on her shoulders.

'Alone at last,' he murmured in her ear.

Turning to him, she put her arms round his neck. He kissed her, and she was immediately lost to everything but the growing fire of desire deep down inside her, a need that rose like an insatiable roaring tide. The force of her longing brought a rush of colour to her cheeks as he released her and she looked away, overcome by her own wantonness.

She waited, half eager, half afraid that he might suggest taking her up to her room or make some sort of overture, but Craig looked at her flushed cheeks and his mouth thinned. 'Why don't *we* go out to lunch?' he said rather abruptly.

Charlotte stiffened. 'Yes, why not?' she agreed, over-brightly. 'I'll go and get ready.' And she ran out of the study, taking the stone stairs two at a time in her haste to get to her room and shut herself away with her disappointment.

But when she came out to join Craig twenty minutes later she had managed to hide her feelings enough to laugh and chatter with him as they drove to a pub for lunch. He looked at her approvingly and encouraged her to talk, pleased at her returning animation. He had phoned ahead to book a table and they both did full justice to the slices of rare beef that the chef cut for them from the huge roast on its silver serving dish.

'I'm glad I got you out of the house,' Craig smiled at her. 'You're starting to look better already.'

'It isn't the house,' Charlotte answered. 'I love the house. It just seems so empty without my father and Renate.'

'And over-full when Verity's there,' Craig supplied when she hesitated to go on. 'You've got to learn to stand up to her, you know,' he urged gently. 'You've as much right to decide what happens to the house as she has.' He looked at her musingly. 'You're a different person when she's around. You seem to lose all your vitality and...' He hesitated, seeking the right word.

'Sophistication?' Charlotte suggested wryly. 'I'm afraid I'm not, very. Not compared to Verity, anyway. I try to be, but...'

'My dear girl!' Craig took hold of her hand. 'Do you think I don't know? Verity was born sophisticated. But you're far more open and natural. And much more sensitive, I should think. You're a gentle breeze to her devastating tornado.'

Charlotte listened to his opinion of her with mixed emotions. Nice to be called natural and sensitive, she supposed, but she wanted to make far more of an impact on him than a gentle breeze! Her appetite suddenly gone, she pushed her plate away. 'Must we talk about Verity?' she said irritably. 'Even when you're away from her you can't stop talking about her.' Think about me, her heart cried out. We could have been together now, close like we used to be, instead of sitting here arguing about Verity. It's always *her* and not *me*!

Craig was looking at her in surprise. 'Only because of the effect she seems to have on you. Why do you two dislike each other so much?'

'We're sisters,' she answered shortly. 'Are you—are you going to take her to London with you?'

'Now who's talking about her?' He shrugged. 'Yes, I suppose so. It would be rather odd not to, wouldn't it? But I shall drop her off at a hotel, if that's what you're worrying about,' he said shortly. He ran his hand across his forehead, pushing a dark lock aside. 'Will you go back to work next week?'

'Yes. I've had quite a lot of time off already.'

'I still don't like the idea of you being alone in that great house. Can't you close it up and go and stay with a friend? Or have a friend come and stay with you?'

'Perhaps. I'll see what I can do.' She hesitated and then said in a rather strained voice, 'It's kind of you to—to worry about me.' Craig shook off her thanks and Charlotte looked at him sadly, thinking how much they had grown apart since her father's illness, such a short time ago. They seemed to be being pushed farther and farther apart. And there was nothing she could do to stop it. She wanted him so much, and yet she found it impossible to tell him so. The opportunity had been there this morning; when he'd suggested going out to lunch, she could have said no, let's stay. But how could she have done when he seemed so uninterested? But then, who would notice a breeze when there was a tornado blowing? she thought bitterly.

'You're looking sad again,' Craig chided her. 'What would you like to do this afternoon?'

She managed to laugh. 'It's pouring with rain still; a typical English summer afternoon. And Sunday, too. Which doesn't give us very much choice.'

'No.' He raised an eyebrow. 'A film?'

'OK—a film.'

So they spent the afternoon in a cinema, watching a modern love story that contained a scene that was so erotic it made Charlotte's throat go dry with frustration and her body feel achingly empty inside. She couldn't look at Craig, couldn't hold his hand tightly, even though she wanted to so desperately. She could only sit in her seat with her hands twisting together in her lap under the cover of her coat, wishing for what might have been.

When they came out of the cinema it was still raining and there was nothing to do but go back to the Abbey. Charlotte had a feeble hope that Verity might still be out so that Craig and she would have some time alone, even though there seemed little enough to hope for now. But her sister was already home and in a bad mood.

'Where did you two go? I've been packed and ready to leave for ages!'

'We had lunch out and went to see a film,' Charlotte answered.

'You might have told me you were going. I expected you to be here,' Verity complained. 'Lord, I can't wait to get back to civilisation! Do be a dear and hurry, Craig. I'd like to get to London as early as possible.'

So there was no time for anything but hurried goodbyes. Craig kissed Charlotte with Verity waiting in the car and said, 'I'll phone you tomorrow. And remember what I said—try and get someone to stay with you. Tonight if you can. Goodnight, Charlie.' His eyes were intent on her face for a moment and he bent to kiss her lightly on the cheek, but then his arm went round her waist and he pulled her against him as he kissed her hard on the mouth, as if daring her to defy him. But, before she could put her arms around him and return the kiss, Craig abruptly let her go and strode quickly to the car.

Charlotte watched them go and listened to the noise of the car's engine fading, leaving behind an empty silence that seemed to stretch interminably into the future. Slowly she closed the heavy door, bolted it and went up to lie in her lonely bed, filled with an immense sense of loss, torturing herself with thoughts of Verity and Craig alone in the car, a time that she was quite sure Verity would make the most of.

True to his promise, Craig rang the next evening, but he was in a hurry, on his way to have dinner with a client, he said, and couldn't talk for very long. Had really only rung to check that she was all right and to tell her that he had to go to Manchester for a couple of days, so she wouldn't be able to get in touch with him.

The next evening Charlotte had to work late to catch up on the backlog that had built up while she'd been away and so missed Craig's call, and the following evening came back into the house from seeing to the horses just as the phone stopped ringing. The next two nights he didn't call. The phone did ring on Friday evening and she ran to answer it, but it was only Verity, saying she would be down the next day.

Charlotte was kept busy sorting through her father's things and deciding which furniture to send for auction. Early on Saturday morning a van arrived from the local auctioneers to take away all that she had got ready. It took a couple of hours to load it, and just as it was going through the arched gateway, it met another car that had to back across the bridge to let it pass. Standing on the top of the stone steps, Charlotte waited until the car could pull into the courtyard, and felt no surprise when she saw that Craig had brought her sister.

'Hello.' He got out of the car and strolled over to her, tall and so good-looking in black riding trousers, white sweater and lightweight jacket, a scarf thrown casually round his neck. 'Have you been staying with someone? I couldn't reach you.'

'No. We must have missed each other.' He put his hands on her arms and bent to kiss her, but Charlotte turned her head so that he could only reach her cheek. His hands tightened for a moment and when she looked at him his face was drawn into a tight mask.

'We've got something to show you,' Verity told her as soon as she walked into the house. 'Craig has drawn up the plans for the house, and he's sent a copy to a friend of his on the local planning committee. So it shouldn't be too long before we get permission to go ahead,' she added with satisfaction.

'Subject to your approving the plans, of course, Charlie.' But, although he included her, Craig's voice was cool and withdrawn.

For ten minutes or so they went over the plans, with Verity doing most of the talking. Craig had done a brilliant job, even a layman like Charlotte could see that, incorporating all the unusual architectural features of the house into the conversion. He had even done specimen drawings of some of the rooms, showing how they looked now and through the various stages of conversion to the finished product.

'You must have put a lot of time into this,' she remarked, looking at Craig.

'I had two nights in a hotel in Manchester to kill. Are you satisfied with the plans?'

'Yes. They're—they're very good.'

'I knew you'd agree,' Verity joined in. 'So I went to a solicitor and had this agreement drawn up. It details how we'll split up the proceeds from the sale of the flats.'

'You don't waste any time,' Charlotte observed coldly.

'What's the point in doing that? You've just got to read it, and then all three of us sign it.'

Charlotte took the document, but said, 'What about Craig? Don't you think you ought to have consulted him first? After all...'

'Craig's already seen it,' Verity interrupted. 'In fact, we got together and thrashed it out before I went to the solicitor,' she added in mocking delight. 'You'll find it very fair. And it makes provision in case you change your mind and decide to have one of the flats in lieu of cash. Craig insisted on that. In fact, he insisted on a lot of things for you that I didn't really feel you...'

'Where do I sign?' Charlotte interrupted sharply.

'But you haven't read it yet!'

'You must read it, Charlie.' Craig added his voice to Verity's. 'There may be alterations you want to make.'

'It doesn't matter.' Picking up a pen that Craig had been using, she quickly signed the last page of the agreement. 'There. Now you can go ahead. When do you want me to move out? I can get rid of the rest of the furniture next week and move out by the weekend, I suppose. But I'd like to leave the horses in the paddock until I can find somewhere else for them, if you don't mind.'

'Oh, really, Charlie, don't be so childish!' Verity said insultingly. 'No one's pushing you out. It could be weeks yet, and anyway, you could always move into one of the wings while the main house is being done. In fact, it would probably help to have someone here to make sure that the builders do their work properly.'

'Thank you very much,' Charlotte answered acidly, 'but I really don't feel like staying here to be an unpaid foreman while I watch my home being torn apart. Do your own dirty work for once, Verity!' And she marched out of the room, bright spots of anger on her cheeks.

Craig came to look for her ten minutes later and found her sitting in the kitchen garden, her back against the wall, the sun drying the wetness of tears on her cheeks. She looked up as his shadow loomed over her, but then quickly lowered her head.

Sitting down beside her on the grass, Craig said, 'I'm riding in a race this afternoon. Want to come and watch?' She shook her head and he glanced at her set profile for a moment before saying, 'I tried to reach you to tell you about the agreement and ask your opinion, but I couldn't get hold of you, so I thought it better to go through it with Verity rather than let her have her head and have to argue her into altering it all.'

'Did it take much—discussion?'

'Quite a lot.' Craig grinned wryly. 'Verity's become quite a sharp little businesswoman.'

'And where did your discussions take place? At her place or yours?'

'Charlie, I——'

She got angrily to her feet. 'And did you discuss old times, too? I bet you did. I bet Verity wouldn't let an opportunity like that slip by!'

'Charlie, for heaven's sake!' Craig stood and caught her arm. 'What is this? Don't you listen to me? I'm not interested in Verity any more.'

'But you saw her in London. How many times? Once? Twice? Or even more? Did you take her out to dinner?' He was silent, standing tight-lipped, and she said bitterly, 'There you are, you did! And did you go back to her room with her? Did you make love to my sexy sister?'

Suddenly Craig was shaking her, unable to control his anger. 'No, I damn well didn't! Because I happen to care about you.'

'But you had the opportunity. She wanted to go to bed with you, didn't she? *Didn't she*?'

Instead of the longed-for denial, Craig said roughly, 'You don't know what you're saying.' Gritting his teeth, he took a firm hold of himself and said more gently, 'Look, Charlie, you're overwrought. You haven't been yourself since your father was taken ill. That's understandable. But this thing you've got about Verity and me... Can't you see that it's pushing us apart? Since she's been here you've changed completely.'

'Because I know that she always get what she wants. And she wants you!'

'That's ridiculous. It was over for both of us years ago.'

'But she will—I know she will.'

'Why? Why are you so sure?'

'Because...' Charlotte's voice broke on a sob. 'Because you're mine, and Verity always takes what's mine. She always has.'

Craig stared down at her, frowning in anger. 'And do you think I have no say in the matter?'

'No.' She shook her head wretchedly. 'I told you; Verity always gets what she wants.'

His mouth thinning, Craig said grimly, 'Well, thanks for the vote of confidence. Don't you have any belief in what I say? Any trust in me? Because if you haven't, I might as well walk out of here and never come back. Let Verity find someone else to convert the house. Is that what you want, Charlie? *Is it?*'

He had taken her wrists and gripped them hard as he spoke, his fingers digging into her. She winced a little but slowly shook her head. 'No, I... No.'

His fingers relaxed, but he said roughly, 'Then for God's sake stop this. Do you understand, Charlie? It has to stop. I've been as patient with you as I know how. I've respected your grief—or what I thought was your grief—but I can't take any more of this ridiculous jealousy. Especially when there's absolutely no reason for it.'

She was silent, her body trembling, and Craig put his arms round her and drew her to him to kiss her on the forehead. 'Now,' he said softly, 'why don't you go and change and we'll drive out to the racecourse? You can watch me ride, and then we'll have a bottle of champagne to celebrate my win, and afterwards we'll go out to dinner.'

'Just the two of us?'

'Just the two of us,' he confirmed.

'What if you lose?'

'Then we'll have two bottles of champagne to commiserate.'

They had a wonderful afternoon, and only needed one bottle of champagne because Craig won easily. It was time out, a reprieve from doubts and fears, and it felt so marvellous to have Craig to herself, both at the racecourse and afterwards at the candlelit restaurant where they had dinner. Or it was until Charlotte spoiled it all. Craig had apologised because he was going to be busy the following week and wouldn't be able to get down to see her, so Charlotte said, 'Couldn't I meet you in London one evening?'

'Well, I've got rather a lot on, I'm afraid.'

'Have you?' Her face tightened and before she could stop herself she found herself saying, 'But you managed to find plenty of time to see Verity!'

'For God's sake!' His face grim, Craig stood up. 'Let's go.'

They sat silently in the car on the ride home. Charlotte was furious with herself and wanted to apologise, but Craig's profile was granite-hard and her heart failed her. When he kisses me goodnight, she thought, then I'll tell him.

But when they got back to the house the light was on in the sitting-room and they could hear the sound of a record player, so they knew Verity was home. She was lying on the sofa, her feet propped up on the arm, and was wearing a low-necked evening dress that had got tucked under her, revealing a long length of very shapely legs in black stockings. There was a glass in her hand and an almost empty bottle of wine on the floor beside her. Charlotte looked at her in surprise. 'Didn't you go out?'

'Yes. A director of the local radio station took me out to dinner, but I found him eminently boring, so I pleaded a headache.' She patted the sofa. 'Come over here, Craig, my sweet, and tell me all about your race. And bring a glass, let's make a night of it. It will be like old times.'

Craig glanced at Charlotte and what he saw in her face made his lips thin sardonically. Picking up a glass, he went over to sit beside Verity, his dark eyes throwing Charlotte a definite challenge. 'Why not?' he said shortly.

Charlotte stood there for a moment, staring at them and not trusting herself to speak, then she turned and ran up to her room.

But once there she realised how foolish she had been, how she had let Verity gain the upper hand again—and so easily. Craig had said that she must trust him and she wanted to, wanted it more than anything else in the world, but did he have to test that trust now, when it made such a victory for her sister? Slowly she showered and put on a nightdress, then pushed open the window to look out while she brushed her hair. The stars shone in the clear sky, but were almost drowned in the brilliant radiance of the full moon. A great surge of longing filled her heart and she knew that she had to put this right with Craig, and must do it now.

Pulling on a robe, she ran down to the sitting-room, not caring that Verity might laugh at her, but she found the room empty, the record playing to itself. She stared at the empty room in consternation, her mind already filling with suspicion and distrust. Turning, she ran into the outer hall and saw that the front door was not only unlocked but stood open. She ran on into the courtyard, under the gatehouse and across the bridge, the swirling skirts of her long white nightdress making her look like some supernatural spirit reflected in the waters of the moat.

The broken walls of the ruins spread before her and she ran through them, her bare feet making no sound on the grass. Then she saw them, together in the moonlight. Craig had Verity in his arms and was carrying her. As Charlotte watched, Verity put her arms round his neck and they began to kiss. Charlotte's hand went to her mouth as she gave a cry of pain and revulsion. But Craig heard and he raised his head to stare at her. She expected him to speak, to say something, but he didn't. Suddenly Charlotte was filled with an overwhelming fury and an uncontrollable need to hit back at him for this terrible pain in her heart. 'Take her, then!' she yelled at him. 'You deserve one another. Oh, God, how I hate you!'

CHAPTER SIX

CHARLOTTE spent the rest of that night in her room with the door locked, the windows shut and the curtains tightly drawn, but she still couldn't shut out what she'd seen, and what, in her imagination, she could still see Craig and Verity doing together. Craig didn't come to her door, trying to give an explanation, and she didn't expect him to. After all, what explanation could there possibly be except the obvious one—that he had fallen victim to her sister's sensuality all over again? She dozed on and off, and in the morning she got up and put on clean jeans and a white shirt with a navy sweater over it. Her hair she pulled back and tied severely at her neck, but several small curls escaped to soften the harsh effect.

Going out to the paddock, she saddled the mare and went for a long ride, not returning until the morning was almost over.

Craig was waiting for her, sitting on the paddock gate in the sun. He was stripped to the waist, his already tanned body drawing her eyes. He swung down from the gate and held it open, his eyes on her cold face. Charlotte dismounted and he came to take off the saddle for her, but she said sharply, 'I can manage, thanks,' and did the job herself.

Deliberately she turned and began to walk away from him, but Craig caught her arm and pulled her round to face him. 'I want to talk to you,' he said grimly.

'You're mistaken,' she snapped back icily. 'We have nothing to say to each other.'

'Well, maybe you don't, but I have. And you're going to listen whether you like it or not,' he added as Charlotte went to put her hands over her ears, and he pulled them down, holding on to her wrists.

'You can't make me. Do you think I want to hear any more of your lies?'

'Shut up!' The fury in his voice cut her off, for a moment making her feel afraid. 'I'm going to say this just once and you're going to listen. Whether you believe me or not is up to you. I'm getting so I frankly don't care much either way.' He glared at her, his temper held under a short rein. 'Whatever that warped mind of yours thought last night, I was only carrying Verity back to the house. When you flounced off to bed I felt damn fed up, so I decided to go for a walk.'

Charlotte shot him a venomous look at that and tried to pull away, but he held her still. 'Verity followed me outside. She was drunk,' he said bluntly. 'And upset about something. She kept on about expecting a call from the States that hadn't come. I suppose you could say she was maudlin. She kept following me about and trying to scramble over the ruins in her high heels until I was afraid she'd break an ankle. I was fed up with her, too. She was the last person I...' He broke off, then after a moment said shortly, 'In the end I just picked her up to carry her back to the house. And that was when you came along.'

'Yes,' Charlotte agreed caustically. 'That was when I came along. Just as you were kissing her.'

'As she was kissing *me*.' Craig corrected, his face hardening.

'Oh, I do beg your pardon,' Charlotte answered with sarcastic politeness. 'And weren't you the one who said you had some say in the matter?'

A bleak look came into his eyes. 'I'm not going to argue about it, Charlie.'

She looked up at him, her face white. 'If what you say is true, you didn't have to help her.'

'Don't be silly, of course I did. She could have fallen and hurt herself.' His hand tightened on her wrists. 'I'm not going to ignore Verity just because of your jealousy, Charlie. She's your sister, she's a business partner now, and she's an old friend. I'm...'

'An old flame, you mean,' Charlotte cut in, her anger rising again. 'Or was she more than that? If you can go back to her so easily, then...'

'I have *not* gone back to her!' His own temper mounting, Craig pushed her away as if he couldn't trust himself not to hurt her in his anger. 'And for the last time—we were not lovers!'

'But Verity says *you were*. Who am I supposed to believe?'

The hard line of Craig's jaw thrust forward as he said, 'Well, you'll just have to work that out for yourself, won't you?'

'I want to believe you, but...'

'Do you? I doubt it.' He glared at her angrily. 'You're as obsessed about Verity as your father was,' he said harshly. 'But in entirely the opposite way. Did it ever occur to you that that's why you're so jealous of her—because your father doted on her so much?'

'Maybe I was,' Charlotte admitted. 'But that's in the past. It's you—I'm so afraid that she'll take you away from me.'

'She could never do that,' he answered shortly. 'But the way you're behaving—don't you see that *you're* driving me away? How can we have any kind of relationship when you don't even trust me? You won't even take my word for it that I never made love to Verity. What the hell hope for the future have we got when you're so damn suspicious?'

He glanced at her for a moment, then turned abruptly on his heel and began to stride towards the house.

'Craig, where are you going?' Charlotte ran after him and caught his sleeve.

'Back to London. There certainly doesn't seem to be anything to keep me here.'

'No, don't go like this, please! I'm sorry. I...'

'Charlie,' Craig turned impatiently to face her, 'I don't want it to be like this, either. But it's up to you. You've got to make up your mind to trust me. Until you do...'

'Craig!' Verity's voice cut into their argument as she called him from the bridge, 'Hey, I'm ready to go!'

Charlotte's body grew tense. 'You're leaving now—with her?'

Craig's eyes narrowed warningly. 'I said I'd take her back with me, yes. But if...'

But he had no time to finish as Charlotte stepped away from him and said viciously, 'Go, then. Don't let *me* keep you. In London you'll be able to see her as often as you like. And maybe while you're there you'll make up your mind just which one of us you want!'

Craig's face darkened furiously. He took a half step towards her, his hand outstretched, but then swore and strode angrily away to where Verity was waiting for him. Verity smiled, but he went right past her into the courtyard. She went running after him, and five minutes later Craig's car came out of the Abbey and drove off fast down the road.

For the next terrible week Charlotte heard nothing from either of them, then she got a letter from an official surveyor saying he wanted to go over the house before passing the plans, and making an appointment to do so. At the end he said he had asked the architect, Mr Craig Bishop, to be present. Charlotte rang the surveyors' office to confirm the appointment and told them that they would have to get the key from her nearest neighbour as she would be at work.

When the day came she wasn't able to concentrate on her work, her mind full of thoughts of Craig being so near, of him going over the house with the surveyor, and of him going into her own bedroom. Would he think of her then? Or would he go into Verity's room and think of her instead? Charlotte tried to shake off the festering suspicions, but there was no getting away from the torturing pictures her imagination painted for her.

The surveyor had arranged to meet Craig at the house at eleven that morning, so when Charlotte drove home at five-thirty she was quite confident that they would be long gone. But when she drove into the courtyard Craig's car was still there. For a wild moment she thought of driving away again, but realised Craig would have heard her arrive. Slowly she got out and let herself into the house. Craig was sitting in the deep window-seat of the drawing-room, one leg up on the seat, a glass in his hand. He didn't get up when she came in, just looked her over assessingly, as if trying to gauge what kind of mood she was in.

'I helped myself to a drink; I hope you don't mind,' he said with icy politeness.

'No. No, of course not.' Charlotte put her bag down on a chair and couldn't find anything to say.

'I see you got rid of a lot more furniture,' Craig remarked, his eyes travelling round the almost empty room and settling on her again.

'Yes, there didn't seem any point in waiting.' She waited for him to go on but, when he didn't, said, 'How did you get on with the surveyor?'

'He has a few modifications that he wants done, from the safety aspect mostly, but otherwise he's quite satisfied. We should get an official letter shortly and then we can go ahead.'

'I see. So—what do you want me to do?'

Putting down his glass, Craig got up and crossed to his briefcase. He took some plans from it and spread them out on the one small table left in the room. 'First I'd better show you the modifications.'

He looked at her expectantly and Charlotte slowly moved over to stand beside him. He began to point out the alterations, but she didn't listen, only nodded whenever he paused. She was so terrible aware of him— of his broad shoulders in the well-cut business suit, of his strong hands as he pointed out the plans, of his deep authoritative voice, and of the faint but evocative smell of musky aftershave. Sensual desire ran through her veins like a wave of molten lava, a feeling so strong that her body began to tremble and she had to move away for fear that Craig would notice.

'I'm sorry,' he said shortly. 'I should have remembered you have no interest in any of this.'

'I have. I just...' Her nails digging into her palms, she turned to face him. 'What happens next?'

Craig's eyes narrowed as they ran over her. 'I've already asked two or three building firms for estimates. They'll want to see over the house, and I shall probably have to go over it with them. And once work starts, of course, I'll be down here as often as I can to make sure that everything is going smoothly. But if there are any problems you'll have to get in touch with me.' He paused, his eyes on her lowered face. 'So one way or another it seems we're going to see quite a lot of each other in the near future.'

His voice was withdrawn, almost speculative, and Charlotte sensed that he was in a strange mood. Her heart had started to beat painfully and she longed to reach out and touch him, to have him take her in his arms. But she couldn't, not any more. She'd forfeited that right—if she had ever really had it at all. 'What about Verity?' she asked stiffly. 'Will she be coming down here to stay any more?'

Craig gave a mirthless laugh and thrust his hands into the pockets of his trousers, stretching the material across his hips. 'I have no idea what Verity is doing or is going to do. I haven't seen her since the last time we were here. Not since I dropped her off at her hotel that night. Not that I expect you to believe me. You're too much of a masochist for that,' he added acidly.

Charlotte's head came up and she stared at him, her grey eyes wide in her set face. 'I'm not. I...' She bit her lip. 'Do you think I'm *enjoying* this?'

'Aren't you?'

She shook her head wretchedly. 'No, of course not.'

Craig studied her face for a moment. 'No, I don't suppose you are. But you still believe all those things you levelled at me. All that rubbish about me still wanting Verity.'

'Was it—rubbish?'

'Hell's teeth!' He suddenly turned and smashed his fist against the wooden panelling of the wall, a blow so violent that a picture shook and fell off its hook, crashing to the floor. He turned on her, his face white, jaw clenched. 'How many times do I have to tell you? What do I have to do to prove it to you?'

'You could...' Charlotte took a deep breath. 'You could show me that you...' Her voice faded as she gazed up at him, her eyes wide and vulnerable, a pleading yearning for reassurance in their grey depths.

Craig gazed at her for moment, a pulse beating in his throat, then he slowly reached out and put his hand on her shoulder and drew her roughly to him. 'Come here, then.'

She had tied her hair in a bow at the back of her neck, but he untied it so that her hair fell about her shoulders. One lock fell forward on to her cheek and he brushed it away. Their eyes held, hers still heavy with longing and in Craig's a strange mixture of desire and doubt. But when he bent to kiss her his lips were hard and demanding, awakening an instant response. Charlotte gave a low moan of thankfulness and put her arms around his neck, her body close to his as she kissed him avidly, hungry to be held and kissed and loved.

'Craig! Oh, Craig, I've missed you so much!' She moved against him, her body already stirred by deep-down longing.

Craig gave a gasping kind of groan and tightened his hold, desire deepening to fierce passion as he arched her against him and began to kiss her eyes, her throat, returning with raging insistence to her lips.

She made sounds against his mouth, a mixture of half-words and panting gasps as she tried to tell him she loved him, but she was too overcome by emotion to be coherent. Craig put a hand in her hair, his shoulders hunching as she opened her mouth under his, letting him explore with his tongue the warm moistness within. His body trembled and he moved his other hand down on her waist, pressing her against the growing hardness of his body, making tremors of awareness run through her, making her hips gyrate in their own desperate dance of longing.

For a few moments Craig's mouth left hers as he threw his head back and groaned aloud. He gripped her arms, hurting her for a moment, but then his hands were at the buttons of her blouse, almost tearing the material in his haste and hampered by the frantic kisses Charlotte rained on his face. But the last button came free and he pulled it off and tossed it aside, already searching for the fastening of her bra. He undid it with one experienced movement and that too was thrown impatiently aside. He cupped her breasts, holding their fullness in his palms, caressing and fondling them until the sensitive nipples hardened sensuously. Only then did he bend his head to kiss them, starting at the valley between her breasts and slowly working over their soft roundness.

It was wonderful, ecstatic, but Charlotte's nerve-ends were on fire and only one thing would assuage them. She waited breathlessly for him to reach the points of her breasts, but he teased her, coming close but never touching them until she couldn't stand it any longer. 'Please. Oh, Craig, please!' She put her hands in his thick, curly hair, turning his head to where she wanted it. His mouth closed over her nipple and for a few moments it was the most blissful relief, but then his lips began to pull at her, driving her crazy all over again. She gasped and drew back, losing her balance so that she fell to her knees, bringing Craig down with her. He kissed her fiercely on the mouth again and then leaned back to peel off his jacket and pull at his tie. She tried to help him with the buttons of his shirt, but only got in the way, delaying the erotic moment when he pulled her against his broad chest, his hot skin rubbing on hers, driving her into another frenzy of desire.

'Sweetheart—oh, God, sweetheart!' Craig bore her down on to the floor, their bodies gilded by a ray of golden evening sunlight that shone through the arched windows and turned the old threadbare carpet on which they lay into a rich, jewelled bed. He lay half across her, kissing her in a surge of passion, their arms round each other as they rolled on the floor, almost fighting in their urgency to give and be given. As they moved, Charlotte's skirt rode up her legs, and then she felt Craig's hand on her thighs, on the few inches of soft flesh between the tops of her stockings and her panties. His fingers were burning hot, leaving trails of fire on her quivering skin.

He turned her on her back and kissed her fervently, his fingers exploring, probing, making her arch her hips towards him and cry out in abandoned excitement.

But it was too exciting—and yet not enough. Unable to stand it any longer, Charlotte pushed his hand away and reached for him, craving to fill this yearning emptiness deep inside her. Her fumbling, urgent fingers searched for the clasp of his trousers, but his hand closed over hers, holding it prisoner until she grew still and stared up at him with wide, questioning eyes.

He kissed her deeply, but then sat up and pushed his hair back with an unsteady hand.

'Craig?'

She put a hand on his back and let her fingers trail down his spine. He trembled convulsively and slowly turned to look down at her. 'No,' he said shortly, his voice thick and uneven. 'Not like this, Charlie.'

'What—what do you mean?'

'Don't you remember how this started?' he demanded, a harsh note creeping into his voice. 'You wanted me to prove to you that I preferred you to Verity. Is that really how you want me to make love to you the first time—just to spite your sister?' He looked at her, but she didn't speak, just pulled down her skirt as she sat up, then put an arm across her chest in an instinctive gesture as she looked round for her bra. 'Well, is it?' he demanded again.

She looked at him then and slowly shook her head. 'No, I—I suppose not.'

'You suppose! Don't you know?'

Charlotte shook her head rather helplessly. 'I—I'd forgotten about Verity,' she confessed.

A big grin creased Craig's mouth. 'That's the best thing you've said in weeks! Come here.' He pulled her on to his lap and kissed her shoulder. 'I want to make love to you, Charlie, *by God I do*. It was hard as hell to stop just now. But I want it to be for the right reasons. Can you understand that? Not out of jealousy or anger, but because that's what we both want. And in our own time, not because you're putting me through some kind of test. OK?'

She nodded, her eyes still wide with sexual arousal, and stroked her hand across his bare chest.

'Hey,' he said softly in her ear, 'you know what that does to me?'

Charlotte laughed in amusement. 'I ought to, I'm sitting on your lap.'

'Minx!' He gently bit the lobe of her ear. 'We've never been that far before.'

There was a questioning note in his voice which made her put her arms round his neck and say, 'I didn't want you to stop. Oh, Craig!' His lips found her breast and she caught her breath, her fingers digging into his shoulders. When he at length raised his head to look at her, her eyes were dark with longing. 'When?' she said fiercely. 'When will it be the right time?'

CHAPTER SEVEN

THE FOLLOWING Sunday Charlotte went over to the Slaters' house to attend the christening of their new baby, and it was early evening before she got home. Verity was there. A strange car was parked in the courtyard and her sister was up in her old room, sorting through a trunkful of things she had left behind when she went to America.

'Thanks for letting me know you were coming,' Charlotte said drily as she stood in the doorway and looked at the older girl.

'I rang, but you were out.' Verity was kneeling on the floor, delving into the trunk. She pulled out a school photograph, one of those that were about three feet wide. 'Good heavens, I'd forgotten all about this. Didn't we look terrible in our school uniforms?'

Charlotte sat on the bed and watched her. 'Are you staying?'

'Probably not.' Verity sat back on the floor and crossed her legs, looking at Charlotte mockingly.

'So why have you come? Surely not to look through old photographs and things?'

'Why not? I'm deciding what I want to keep.' She paused, being deliberately taunting. 'Or what I want to take back to the States with me.'

'You're going back to America?' Charlotte couldn't keep the eagerness out of her voice, even though she knew she was leaving herself open to Verity's malice.

'Of course. I have my career to think of. And there is—another reason.'

She left the sentence hanging, and Charlotte looked at her narrowly. You could never be sure with Verity; asking a direct question had more often than not led to a snub and being told to mind her own business. But now there was a little smile playing around her mouth and she was looking at Charlotte expectantly. So, reluctantly, Charlotte said, 'What other reason?'

Verity laughed at her mockingly. 'I thought you'd never ask!' A 'cat who'd got the cream' look came into her eyes and she said, 'Actually, I might be getting married before too long.'

'Married!' Charlotte came to her feet, for a moment convinced that she meant Craig, but the triumphant laughter in Verity's face made her realise her mistake and she sat down again, her heart beating painfully. 'You—you mean you're engaged?'

'No, darling, nothing so prosaic,' Verity drawled. 'In Hollywood they don't go in for engagements much; you just wait for the man's divorce to come through and then you marry him fast before he has a chance to relish his freedom and change his mind.'

Charlotte stared at her in horror. 'Are you saying that this man is already married?'

'Yes,' Verity's smile was genuinely pleased. 'He's finally left his wife and he's going to marry me. And he's quite a catch. He's a film director—an American.'

'And you've taken him from his wife, broken up his marriage?' There was shocked reproach in Charlotte's voice. 'That's a terrible thing to do!'

'Rubbish!' Verity gave her an impatient look. 'Happy marriages don't break up. Just the same as men who are in love don't go with other women.' She gave Charlotte a calculating look. 'Men like Craig. He isn't in love with you, you know.'

'You don't know that,' Charlotte retorted, realising now where all this had been leading.

Verity gave one of her tinkling laughs. 'Oh, yes, I do. If you think about it, you'll realise I've just told you why, little sister.'

Charlotte came agitatedly to her feet. 'I don't believe you. Craig hasn't—wouldn't go with other women.'

'Wouldn't he?' Verity uncoiled herself and rose in one lithe, graceful movement. 'No, perhaps that was an exaggeration. I didn't mean other *women*, I meant just one other woman—me.'

'You're lying!' Charlotte snapped, bright spots of angry colour in her cheeks. 'He—he despises you.'

'Maybe he does at that,' Verity admitted. 'But it doesn't stop him from wanting me. He's crazy about me, Charlie. When we're together he can't keep his hands off me. I drive him wild and he just couldn't wait to get me into bed. It was just the same when we first went out together, but then I held him off. This time...' She deliberately paused, twisting the knife. 'This time even I couldn't hold him off any longer.' She smiled reminiscently. 'And I'm glad I didn't. Boy, is he hot stuff in bed! After a night with him I...'

'Shut up!' Charlotte stepped towards her furiously, her hand raised in fierce anger. But then she saw the malevolent triumph in her sister's eyes and somehow managed to control herself, her open hand balling into a clenched fist. 'I don't believe you. You're making it up. You're just trying to goad me into losing my temper.'

'And why should I want to do that?'

'I don't know. But you've always hated me—and I don't know why that is, either.'

'Don't you?' Verity threw her a pouting, moody look. 'Because when Mother was alive she always preferred you, of course. She had no time for me or Daddy after you were born.'

Charlotte stared at her in horror, many things now perfectly clear to her. 'And because of that you've lied to me about Craig?'

'Oh, for God's sake!' Verity rounded on her angrily. 'I'm not lying about him. I made up my mind to take him away from you and I have. It's as simple as that.'

'But you got your way over the house! Surely you . . .'

'It wasn't because of that,' Verity said sharply. 'Or at least that was only the start of it. I decided I wanted him because you were so besotted with him, if you must know. And I found it amusing to pay him back for ditching me all those years ago. Nobody does that to me and gets away with it.'

'But you're in love with someone else.'

'In love? Oh, you mean Steve, my film director.' Verity gave a gurgle of laughter. 'What a hopeless romantic you are, Charlie! Love doesn't come into it. A girl has to be practical when she's planning her future. And Steve is going to be very helpful in my career.'

'And that's why you've taken him away from his wife—just so that you can get more parts in films?' Charlotte stared at her, aghast.

'And what better reason is there? It's a very cut-throat world in the film business, let me tell you. You need everyone on your side that you can get. And besides,' Verity added impishly, 'his wife was really bitchy to me when we first met, so she deserves everything she's got coming to her.'

Charlotte listened to her with an appalled face. 'You're—you're heartless! Don't you care about anyone or anything?'

'I care about my career—and that's all. And I intend to get to the top before it's too late.'

'Before you get too old, you mean,' Charlotte hit back, guessing the truth. 'That's what you're afraid of, isn't it? Of losing your looks.'

'I'm an actress, not a tennis player,' Verity flashed back. 'And I'm still only twenty-eight. But I want to get to the top while I'm still young—yes, I give you that. And nothing's going to stand in my way.'

'And what happens when this man you're so set on marrying meets someone else, someone younger? When he gets rid of you because he's tired of you?' Charlotte demanded, more out of curiosity than bitchiness. 'He's bound to find out that you don't love him and...'

'No, he won't. I'll make sure of that. And I'll make sure that once he's married to me he'll be so darn satisfied that he'll *never* look at another woman. Unless his films start to flop or a better proposition comes along, of course,' Verity added with a drawl.

Charlotte looked at her sister, realising that she had become so hard that nothing anyone said would make any difference to her. For a moment she felt almost a surge of pity and said, 'I feel sorry for you, Verity. It must be a special kind of hell to go through life without love.'

'Oh, but I can get all the *love* I want,' sneered Verity. 'Including Craig's. Whenever I want it. But don't worry, I'll let you have him back when I've finished with him. Only don't think that you'll ever satisfy him now, because you won't. No one will now that he's had me.'

Charlotte flinched, registering the tense Verity had used, but she said valiantly, 'I still don't believe you. The last time Craig was here we—we came to an understanding.'

'An understanding? How mundane! But he hasn't committed himself to you, has he? And he won't, not while I'm still around. But he'll probably keep you dangling on his line in case I ditch him and he decides to settle for second best. After all, I suppose you might remind him of me.'

Suddenly furiously angry, Charlotte said scornfully, "My God, you're so damn conceited that you think everyone is going to lower themself to your level. Well, Craig isn't like that. And nor am I. And I just hope for your sake, Verity, that you're an extremely good actress, because otherwise your future husband is going to see you for the scheming, sadistic tramp you are and throw you out within a month, if he has any sense. And now will you take what you came for and go?'

'Tut, tut, your claws are showing, little sister,' mocked Verity, in no way put out. 'And all because you're jealous of me and Craig.'

'I am *not* jealous!'' Charlotte spat out. 'Because I don't believe a word of it. Craig told me he didn't want you and I believe *him*—not *you*.'

'Did he now? What a naughty boy, keeping his options open like that. So I suppose he hasn't told you, then, that he asked me to marry him?'

Charlotte had started to make for the door, but Verity's words stopped her dead and she turned to stare at her, white-faced. 'No. No, I—I don't believe you,' she got out after a long moment.

'No? Then why don't you ask him?' Verity taunted. 'Oh, and while you're at it, ask him whether or not he has a scar on his left thigh—his inner thigh. And one that he didn't have when I knew him six years ago. Yes,' she went on, her triumphant eyes fixed on Charlotte's stunned face, 'there's really only one way I could know that, isn't there?'

For Charlotte, the next few days were a living hell. No matter how hard she tried to dismiss Verity's horrible accusations from her mind, they just wouldn't go away. She had arranged with Craig that she would meet him in London at the weekend, but she longed to see him and have the reassurance of his closeness. A hundred times she went to pick up the phone and call him, but somehow restrained herself because she knew that however hard she tried she wouldn't be able to entirely conceal the doubts that Verity had put in her mind all over again. And Craig was no fool, he would guess and accuse her of not trusting him again.

But the things that Verity had thrown at her would be enough to put doubts in anyone's mind, Charlotte thought miserably. Especially those last barbs about Craig asking Verity to marry him—and the most hurtful one about the scar on his thigh. Verity had been so positive, and she couldn't possibly have invented something like that. And she had been equally positive that it was something Charlotte wouldn't know herself. And that hurt. But how could she check it? You couldn't just pick up the phone and ask the man you loved to tell you whether or not he had a scar on his thigh because you wanted to prove whether or not he was having an affair with someone else! At that thought Charlotte began to feel a little hysterical, but then she wanted to burst into tears. She had been so looking forward to seeing Craig on Saturday, and now Verity had ruined all her peace of mind again.

Saturday came at last and Charlotte took the train up to London. Craig had promised to come to the station to meet her and they had arranged to meet by the newsagent's kiosk. Charlotte's train was a little early, but Craig was already there. He had a newspaper in his hands but wasn't reading it with any great concentration; he kept glancing up at the big clock suspended from the roof. For a few minutes Charlotte stood out of sight, watching him, summoning up her courage for this meeting that she'd hoped would lead to a new beginning. Craig looked so tall and handsome, more than one woman gave him a second glance as they passed by, and she felt a little frisson of pride to think that he was waiting for her. He looked at the clock again and then over towards her platform, and Charlotte walked out to where he could see her. Immediately he stiffened, then straightened up as if bracing his shoulders to meet a challenge—or a threat. She wanted to run to him and be held in his arms, but forced herself to walk calmly forward and greet him with an even, 'Hello, Craig.'

'Hello, sweetheart.' He put his hand firmly on her arm and drew her to him to kiss her.

Charlotte returned his kiss, she couldn't help it, but she found herself looking intently into his face to see if there was any guilt there. When she realised what she was doing she quickly drew away, and covered it by laughing and saying, 'Hey, everyone's looking at us!'

'Then let them look,' Craig retorted, kissing her again. 'They're only jealous of me.' He put his arm round her waist and they walked through the station, avoiding the last rush of commuters hurrying to catch their trains.

'How did your trip to Manchester go?' asked Charlotte, trying to keep the conversation away from personal things.

'Very well. We managed to secure three commissions, and one of them is a really large, prestige job.'

He went on talking about the project until they reached his car which was parked in a side road, but once inside it he took her into his arms and said, 'Now, let's say hello properly.'

His kiss was so warm, so possessive, that Charlotte's reserve almost immediately began to melt. She held herself stiffly for only a few moments before her need for him took over and she relaxed against him, returning his kiss. 'Oh, Craig,' she murmured. 'I wish...' She broke off, unable to put her longing into words.

'Mm.' His mouth nuzzled her neck, sending shivers of desire down her spine. 'I know what you mean.' He kissed her again but then drew away reluctantly. 'Hungry?'

'Starving!'

'Good. I've booked a table for seven-thirty. I thought you might like to try something different, so I chose a new wine bar that's recently opened quite near to my flat. I haven't been there myself, but some of my neighbours have and they say it's quite good. The owners have concentrated on the food rather than the décor, which makes a pleasant change. Is that OK?'

'Of course. It sounds fine,' Charlotte agreed warmly, glad that they were going somewhere new, somewhere that Craig couldn't possibly have shared with Verity.

He smiled and put his hand on her knee in a gesture that was both possessive and intimate. 'And I thought that afterwards we could go back to my place—for a nightcap,' he added as an afterthought.

Charlotte was grateful that he'd left the option open for her—or was it just a test to see if she now trusted him? Furious with herself, she pushed the suspicion aside, just as she'd tried to shut out all the anxious fears that Verity had so cruelly planted. Nothing must spoil tonight, nothing. So she smiled back at Craig and moved nearer to him. 'That will be—nice,' she said inadequately.

It didn't take long to reach the restaurant Craig had chosen; the worst of the rush-hour traffic was over and he knew his way through the back streets so well that he was able to avoid any hold-ups.

'Have you lived in London long?' Charlotte asked him. 'You seem so familiar with it.'

'Ever since I left university and started work. It's a great place to live. It has such a marvellous atmosphere, and there's always so much going on.'

He spoke so warmly that Charlotte looked at him curiously. 'But you love the country too, don't you? You said you'd like a house near the Berkshire Downs.'

'That's right.' Craig concentrated on pulling out of the traffic into a parking space. 'But it's possible for a man to love two different places, even to lead two entirely different life-styles.'

And to love two entirely different women? The thought leapt instantly into Charlotte's mind, and she stared at his profile, wondering if it was true. Wondering if she and Verity were so different that he found it possible to want them both; Verity because she was so sophisticated and Charlotte because she fitted in with his more placid, country-loving nature.

'Hey, wake up!'

Craig snapped his fingers and she jumped and blinked. 'What? Oh, sorry, did you say something?'

'Mm, three times. We're here.'

'Oh, are we? I was—I was miles away.'

Craig grimaced. 'I'm already losing my touch,' he said in a mock-woeful voice.

With a laugh, Charlotte leant forward to kiss him lightly. 'No, you're not.'

'Good.' His eyes held hers. 'I was starting to get a bit worried.'

She knew he wasn't talking about now, but about the last few weeks since her father had died—since Verity had been home. Lifting her hand, she gently ran it down his cheek. 'I know. I'm sorry.'

Turning her head slightly, he kissed her palm, his eyes still on her face intently. 'Is everything OK now?'

She nodded, for a moment secure in his closeness. 'Yes, I think so.'

His eyebrows rose a little, but he seemed satisfied. 'Good. Let's go and eat then, shall we?'

They were both pleased with the restaurant. It was small enough to have a warm and friendly atmosphere, but also large enough for the tables to be far enough apart for your conversation not to be overheard. It was already quite full of pre-theatre diners, so they sat in the bar for a while while they waited for a table.

'How have you been?' Craig asked her. 'I worry about you alone in that big house.'

'You shouldn't. I've been fine. And there's always the telephone. If I was worried, I could call a neighbour.'

'And just how far away is the nearest house?'

Charlotte smiled and shrugged. 'All right, so it's nearly half a mile away—but someone would still come.'

'It still worries me.' He turned as the waiter brought their drinks and later said, 'I'm afraid there'll be quite a lot of upheaval once the builders start work. You'll have to move out of the main house into one of the wings for a start.'

'I don't really mind that. And, as you said, it will be useful to have someone there to keep an eye on things.'

'Well, it will probably save me a great deal of time, admittedly.' Craig took a drink and held the glass between his hands as he leaned forward and said, 'Have you changed your mind about having a flat at the Abbey now that you've had more time to think about it?'

Charlotte shook her head. 'No, I don't want to go on living there in those circumstances. I think it will be better to move away and make a fresh start.'

A pleased look came into Craig's eyes. 'I think you're quite right. I know it's a beautiful old place and you love it, but even so I get the impression that you've never been happy there.'

'It was fine when my mother was alive.' She frowned, trying to analyse her feelings. 'Perhaps that's why I was so against changing it; it holds so many memories of my mother. Now they'll all be lost.'

'Not if they're in your heart.'

She gave him a quick glance, wondering who he held in his heart, but then shook her head. 'Memories seem to fade so easily. Especially those you had when you were young. But when I walked round the Abbey I often used to remember my mother—sitting in the window-seat, sewing, or working in the garden. She loved the garden.' For a moment she was silent, thinking of her closeness to her mother in the light of what Verity had said. Had they been too close, shutting out Verity and her father? But then she went on, 'But you're right, after she died I was never so happy again, although it was much better after...' She stopped, realising where she was heading.

But Craig finished the sentence for her. 'After Verity left, you mean. Yes, I imagine it might have.'

Unable to stop herself, Charlotte said, 'She came down last week.'

'Did she?' He seemed in no way put out.

'Yes, she came to sort through the things she'd left behind there. She—she had quite a lot to say, too.'

But Craig didn't seem very interested, which was heartening—or was it just that Verity was too sensitive a subject to talk about?

She sought for the right words to go on, but before she found them Craig had changed the subject, telling her about some new horses that his friends who owned the stables in Berkshire had been given to train. 'The jump racing's almost finished for the summer, so they've asked me to go down any weekend I want and help train them.'

'And will you?'

Craig reached for her hand. 'That rather depends.'

'Oh? What on? This new business project?'

His brown eyes crinkled into a smile and his hand tightened. 'No. On—something quite different.'

The way he looked at her when he said it sent tingles up Charlotte's spine and made her heart start to pound, but even then—at that exciting moment—she thought: is he thinking about me or Verity?

She looked quickly down in case he could read the suspicion in her eyes, and wondered what sadistic demon had entered her mind to torment her so. Somehow she managed to hide her feelings and keep the conversation light while they went to their table, ordered, and began their meal.

'My neighbours were right,' Craig remarked approvingly. 'The food is good.'

'You'll have to come again.'

'*We'll* have to come again,' he commented. 'Often.' He raised his wineglass to clink it against hers. 'To tonight,' he said softly.

Charlotte flushed a little, tried to meet his eyes, but couldn't.

'What is it, Charlie? Is something troubling you?'

For a moment she was tempted to pour it all out, everything that Verity had said, but she imagined the closed, withdrawn look that would come into his face if she did, and she shook her head. 'No. I—I think I'm a little—little nervous, that's all.'

His eyes went swiftly to her face, but after a moment he grinned and said, 'You'd better have some more wine, then.'

'Trying to get me drunk, huh?'

'Of course.' His mouth curled into a mock leer. 'Why else do you think I lured you here?'

He looked so villainous that Charlotte gave a gurgle of laughter, and for a while she relaxed and everything was all right again. Later on, though, some chance remark about the Abbey brought Verity back into her mind. By then they had reached the coffee and mints stage, taking their time as Craig swirled brandy round in a balloon that fitted into his palm. Charlotte sat stirring her coffee, wondering if she dared raise her doubts. She had determined not to because of Craig's insistence that she trust him, but surely it would be better to have everything out in the open and doubts put at rest before they went back to his flat?

'If you stir that much longer, you'll go through the bottom of the cup,' Craig remarked.

'What? Oh, yes.' Hurriedly she put the spoon on the saucer, but couldn't hide the unhappiness in her eyes.

'You'd better tell me,' he said in a resigned tone. 'I suppose it's Verity again?' Charlotte nodded. 'I thought as much. What is it this time?'

'Well, you know I told you Verity came to see me; she—she said that she might be getting married.' As she said it, Charlotte kept her eyes on Craig's face, watching for his reaction, whatever it might be.

But she hadn't at all been expecting a complete lack of any emotion. He merely nodded and said, 'Yes, I know. She told me.'

'She did?' Charlotte gasped in surprise. 'When?'

Craig pursed his lips, thinking back. 'Oh, it must have been over a week ago now.'

'Before last Sunday?'

'Yes, I went to Manchester on the Sunday, so it must have been before then.'

'So she told you before she told me,' said Charlotte with a frown, trying to work out the implications. 'And didn't you—didn't you mind?'

'Mind?' Craig's eyebrows rose. 'No, why should I?'

'Well, you were—fond of her once. Don't some men think that if they can't have a woman then they don't want anyone to have her?'

'Maybe some men do,' he agreed shortly. 'But I don't happen to be one of them. What is this, Charlie?'

Charlotte's face tightened. She wanted to draw back, wishing she'd never started this, but it was too late now. 'Verity said that *you* had asked her to marry you. But it isn't true, is it? She was only lying to make me angry and upset.'

For a moment Craig didn't answer, then he said, 'And did she upset you?'

'Of course,' Charlotte admitted with a short laugh. 'She always manages to do that. Quite easily, in fact.'

'Then don't you think it's about time you stood up to her? The more you let her walk all over you the more she'll do it. You've got to try to...'

'I do,' Charlotte broke in, 'I do try. But—it's difficult. You don't know. You can't understand what it's like to live in—in the shadow of someone like Verity. My father loved her so. Everyone did. *You* did.' Her eyes came up to meet his. 'And you haven't answered my question.'

'No.' Craig's mouth twisted into a grimace. 'Yes, I'm afraid it's true. I was besotted enough over Verity to ask her to marry me once.'

'Once? You mean—when you were going out with her before?'

'Yes, of course. When else?'

Charlotte shook her head rather dazedly and sat back, filled with a great surge of thankfulness. 'But she refused you?'

'No. She obviously wanted to keep her options open. But luckily I saw through her and we had that blazing row and split up. But I'm quite sure she would never have accepted anyway; marriage to me would have been no help at all to her career in films—and I'm sure that that's all she's really interested in.' He gave her a shrewd look. 'I take it Verity didn't tell you *when* I proposed to her?' And when Charlotte shook her head, 'And you, of course, immediately jumped to the wrong conclusion.' He shook his head at her reproachfully. 'Oh, Charlie! What am I going to do with you?'

Charlotte could think of several things she would like him to do to her, and then blushed at her own thoughts. With a low laugh, Craig reached across the table to take her hand. 'Why don't you hurry up and drink that coffee?' he said softly, but with an undertone of urgency that made Charlotte's pulses start to race and drove everything else out of her mind.

'Like that, eh?' she said with a shaky laugh.

'Very much like that.'

She picked up the cup and drank a little, but then put it down again, her hand not quite steady. 'I guess I'm not very thirsty, after all.'

Craig was still holding her other hand, and now he carried it to his lips and gently kissed her fingers, his eyes, darkened by desire, holding hers. A great feeling of love and happiness filled Charlotte's heart, a moment of inner conviction when she knew that she loved Craig completely and that no one else would ever take his place. Without him life wouldn't be worth living; she would go on, but it would never be the same. Craig's hand tightened on hers as he read her feelings clear in her face. 'Let's go,' he said thickly, and turned to beckon the waiter to bring the bill.

The old mansion block where Craig had his flat was only a short distance from the restaurant, but he drove quickly and Charlotte was glad he did because she didn't want this feeling of intense love to fade. She had been to his flat a couple of times before and so didn't feel shy or embarrassed when they walked inside. But it still felt strange knowing that this was the night she'd been waiting for for so long. Ever since that day six years ago when she'd first seen him. Craig took her coat from her, then put his hand behind her neck and drew her to him. His lips were gentle and lingering, kissing her as if it was for the first time, his need for her subjugated under the wish to prolong their lovemaking to its fullest extent, to savour every moment of the night.

Charlotte stood very still in his hold, and yet her senses felt as if they were being drawn into some giddy, spinning whirlpool which was carrying her down, down into a deep chasm of desire. She began to tremble and lifted her hands to grip his shoulders and stop herself from falling as her senses reeled under the impact of his kiss.

'Oh, my little love. My darling!' Craig's lips left her mouth and he began to kiss her throat, working his way down to her shoulder, his hands slipping round to hold her close in his embrace. Still kissing her, he drew her with him out of the hall and into the sitting-room, not bothering to switch on the light, so that only the fused glow of the late evening sun lit them as he stopped, his kiss deepening into passion.

Their senses now were inflamed not only with desire but also with almost unbearable anticipation. Charlotte's trembling body felt hot, so hot. She gave a low moan and moved her hips voluptuously against Craig's, wanting him to assuage this terrible, deep, aching feeling of longing. He groaned and she felt the faint dew of perspiration on his lip. He held her fiercely against him for a moment, but then stepped away, his face taut with need. With a hand that wasn't entirely steady, he began to undo the buttons of her white silk blouse.

The ringing of the doorbell cut harshly through the room, making Charlotte start guiltily and pull away. Craig drew her close again and went on kissing her, but the bell rang for a second time and he groaned and let her go.

'Damn!' He raised a rueful hand to push his hair back from his forehead. 'Sorry. I'll go and see who it is. I won't be a moment.' He walked through into the hall, leaving the sitting-room door ajar, and switched on the light before answering the bell.

Charlotte stayed in the semi-darkness, listening to her heart thudding in her chest, still filled with nervous excitement, but knowing that this was right.

Voices sounded in the hall, first Craig's raised in surprise—and then Verity's. Oh, no! The prayer was fierce and fervent, but it was already too late, as prayers of protest always were. Charlotte's hands immediately went to her blouse as she fumblingly did up the buttons that Craig had undone with such passion. She felt all the heat, all the sensuality drain from her veins, leaving her cold and empty inside, until she swung round to face the door as Verity pushed past Craig and came into the room.

'All in the dark? How romantic!' There was taunting mockery in Verity's voice as she snapped on the light. She was looking very lovely, dressed completely in black with her blonde hair loose and curling softly on her shoulders. As Charlotte looked at her beauty, all the old fears and self-doubts began to return.

'What do you want, Verity?' Craig snapped out.

'I told you, I want to talk to Charlie.'

'Does it have to be now? Can't you make it some other time?'

'Well, I don't see why when I'm already here.' Verity looked round at them both and pretended to give a start of surprise. 'I'm surely not interrupting something, am I? Oh, I do *hope* so!'

Angrily Craig reached out to catch her arm, but she eluded him and walked over to the range of built-in units along the wall. 'I'm so thirsty. Let's have a drink, shall we?' And she opened one of the cupboards to reveal shelves of bottles and glasses. 'We need some lemon slices, darling.' She handed Craig a dish from another shelf. 'Or would you like me to get some? You keep them in the second cupboard along in the kitchen, don't you?'

'All right, Verity,' Charlotte cut in coldly, 'you don't have to spell it out any more. I'm fully aware that you've been here before.'

'Oh. good. Sometimes you can be extremely slow on the uptake, Charlie darling.'

'Why don't you say what you came to say and get out of here?' Craig said to her acidly.

'Tut, tut! How inhospitable you've suddenly become, Craig. It must be Charlie's bad influence. You're usually so—*welcoming*.' She smiled provocatively as she said it, and Charlotte saw Craig's jaw tighten. In anger, she presumed; but was it because Verity had barged her way in or because he was afraid she would say too much? Or was it because he still wanted Verity and couldn't have her now that she was going to marry someone else?

Charlotte suddenly realised how her mind was working and put on her mental brakes hard, appalled that such bleak thoughts should already be going through her head when only a few minutes ago she had been more than ready to consummate her love for Craig. And he for her? But he hadn't actually come right out and said that he loved her, even though he'd called her his love. But that might only have been desire.

Verity put her hands on Craig's arms and leaned close to whisper something in his ear, but he shook her off and stepped away, quite obviously angry now. 'Either speak to Charlie or go,' he told her forcefully.

'All right. But I'd like to talk to her in private, please.'

'No!' Charlotte broke in, instinctively afraid of Verity's poison. 'I—I don't have any secrets from Craig.'

She was rewarded with a quick, warm glance of approval from Craig, but Verity said in an affected tone, 'Don't you? How sweet! Such a shame we can't say the same about him.'

'Just what are you driving at, Verity?' snapped Craig.

But Verity walked across to Charlotte and said in a low voice, 'Well, have you asked him yet?'

Charlotte knew full well what she meant, but in a last valiant effort her chin came up and she said, 'I don't need to ask him. I trust him.'

'Then you're a fool,' Verity said sharply. 'Haven't you learnt yet that men can never be trusted—especially when they've been rejected?' A contemptuous look came into her eyes, but she kept her voice low. 'Why else do you think he's turned to you? Not that I believe you. If you really trusted him you wouldn't be afraid to ask.'

'Go away, Verity! Go away and leave us in peace!'

'Yes, why don't you?' Craig had come up and put his hand on Charlotte's arm, drawing her away.

'OK, OK, I can see when I'm not wanted,' Verity said, lifting her arms in a gesture of placation. 'I'll go—just as soon as Charlie asks you a certain question.'

'What question?' demanded Craig.

'No, it doesn't matter. I don't care,' Charlotte protested desperately.

'Of course it does. If you don't ask him, I will,' Verity threatened.

'For God's sake, what question?'

'Charlie wants to know if you have a scar on your left—er—leg?'

Craig looked from one to the other of them with a frown and didn't answer, so Verity said, 'It's no use prevaricating, Craig. It's the first thing she'd going to look for when you take her to bed,' she added crudely.

His eyes settled on Charlotte's face. 'Yes, I have a scar,' he said heavily.

'Good. Next question, Charlie. Oh, all right, I'll ask it for you, then. When did you get this scar, Craig darling?'

'A couple of years ago. I was thrown in a race and a horse trod on me.' His eyes were still on Charlotte, but she had dropped hers now, all hope gone and quite unable to look at him.

'There, you see, that wasn't difficult, was it, Charlie?' Verity gave her humourless little laugh. 'And now you can have him, darling. I told you I'd give him to you when I'd finished with him, didn't I? But I wanted you to be quite sure you knew exactly what you were getting, because I...'

Her words were cut off as Craig grabbed her by the arm and jerked her away from Charlotte. His face enraged, he marched her into the hall, so fast that Verity almost had to run to keep up. 'Get out, you vicious little cat!' he gritted furiously as he pushed her out the door. 'Get out and stay out!' And he slammed the door shut behind her.

He stood at the door for a moment, rubbing his hands together as if cleansing them of something dirty, then he turned quickly and strode back into the sitting-room, where Charlotte was already putting on her coat.

'What are you doing?'

'Going home,' Charlotte replied tonelessly.

'Running away, you mean. Charlie, can't you see that if you leave now Verity will have won? I've told you time and again that she means nothing to me now, and yet you still let her poison your mind and come between us.'

'She always wins. She always has and always will.'

'Only if you let her.' Craig took hold of her arms and gave her a fierce, angry shake. 'Look, if it's about her seeing my scar, I can explain that. She came here once when I'd just had a shower and...'

'No, I don't want to hear.' Charlotte pulled herself free. 'Can't you see it doesn't matter? She's spoiled everything for us. We could never be happy now. She would always be between us.'

'Of course we could! If only you'd have confidence in yourself and trust in me. All this is only in your mind, Charlie. Nothing happened between Verity and me...'

But Charlotte was already making for the door, her face white and strained.

'Very well, go, then!' Craig shouted after her in frustrated fury. 'Because unless you learn not only to trust me but your own heart, then there certainly is no future for us!'

His words jarred her and Charlotte turned to look at him while he held his breath, but then she shook her head and ran out of the flat.

CHAPTER EIGHT

IT WOULD have been better to make a clean break, but that was impossible when Craig was to be in charge of the development of the house. For the next couple of weeks, though, Charlotte only heard from him through his secretary. But the plans for the alterations had been passed and Craig went round the house with various builders' representatives, but he had his own key and only came when she was at work, so she didn't see him. The day approached when the builders were to start, but before they did so Charlotte had to move out of her room and into another in one of the wings. This was attached to the house, but the doors to it were to be blocked off as soon as the builders started and it was to be left until the first flats were sold. Charlotte spent some time getting the room ready as it had hardly been used for years and the damp had got in, but once it had been dried out it was adequate enough.

It was about this time that she ran into Mike Brooks in the town one Saturday morning. She had hardly seen him since she had started going out with Craig, but he invited her to join him for lunch in the pub near the market square. They talked with the ease of old friends, Charlotte telling him all about the development. She didn't mention Craig, but it was pretty obvious that her time was her own, and Mike soon offered to come over and help her to move the rest of the furniture that she wanted to keep. For a moment she hesitated, wondering whether to accept, but Mike said, 'If I remember rightly you've got some quite heavy stuff, so perhaps I'd better bring a couple of friends from the rugby club to give me a hand.'

So that was OK. Charlotte accepted gratefully and made a mental note to get in some cans of beer for them—quite a few, if her experience of rugby players was anything to go by!

They came over on the Saturday; the builders were due to start on the Monday. Mike's two friends brought their girlfriends with them and it turned into quite a party, but the furniture eventually got moved and they had a barbecue out on the lawn and danced until well past midnight. Charlotte expected to sleep late, and set her alarm clock for seven to be up before the builders arrived. But perhaps it was the strange room, for she woke when the first birds began to sing their welcome to the new day, and found it impossible to go to sleep again. She dressed, but didn't feel like eating, so instead she went into the main part of the house and began to wander round the empty rooms. They all held so many memories, some good, some bad, but all part of her precious childhood. She remembered her father, and her mother before she died, in those few years of happiness which they had had together. Did their spirits roam these rooms? she wondered. Were they angry that their home was going to be broken up? She was sure her father would be furious if he knew. Charlotte wandered into the big room that had once been the Abbot's dining-room, and tried to guess how the dozens of Abbots who had been master here would feel. Going to the fireplace, she put her hand on the worn stone carvings, running her fingers over the fierce dogs, the hart and the foresters in the hunting scene, just as she had so often as a child. Her mind was full of the stories she had made up about them—and had often given herself nightmares because of it!

A step sounded in the open doorway and she twisted round to see Craig standing there. He must have let himself in with the spare key. He seemed equally startled to see her and hesitated in the doorway, almost looking as if he might go away again. But then he saw the tears in Charlotte's eyes and said harshly, 'I'm sorry. I—— Are you all right?'

'Yes.' She nodded and wiped her eyes with her fingers, like a child. 'I was just saying goodbye, that's all.'

'Goodbye?'

'To the Abbey as I knew it,' she answered with an ironical smile.

'This will be a trying time for you,' Craig said abruptly. 'Perhaps it would be better if you moved out completely.'

'I can't do that—I have to earn my share of the profits,' she reminded him cynically. He was still standing in the doorway, almost as if he was afraid to come closer to her. There was a pinched look about his mouth and his eyes had lost their keen vitality. 'Are *you* all right?' she asked awkwardly.

He stiffened. 'Yes, of course. I've just been extremely busy, that's all.' He gave an angry kind of sigh. 'I was going to leave a letter for you, telling you what the builders will be doing this week. I shall leave you a letter every week, and if you have any problems you can tell my secretary and I'll get in touch with the builders and deal with them.'

'I see,' Charlie said woodenly.

He turned on her in sudden anger. 'For God's sake, Charlie! You're not making this any easier. I thought it would be better for both of us if we saw as little of each other as possible. If we didn't see each other at all, in fact. It would give us time to forget.'

The sun had risen enough to shine into the courtyard over the surrounding buildings, and a shaft of light came through the mullioned window where Craig was standing. It laid its mottled rays on him, and Charlotte thought she would never forget how he looked at that moment.

With the sun came the first of the builders' lorries, rumbling noisily over the cobbles of the courtyard. Craig started, as if he had forgotten the world outside, and took an envelope from his pocket. 'Here's the letter I meant to leave for you.' He put it on the windowsill, not wanting to run the risk of touching her, and said abruptly, 'I'll go and meet them, make sure they've got their instructions right.' And he turned and strode from the room without a backward glance.

He was gone by the time Charlotte left for work, and she didn't see him again to speak to for some time. He came to the house, of course, Charlotte knew because the builders mentioned it, but he made a point of coming when she was at work. The builders were so noisy that Charlotte was glad to escape to work, but she made a point of seeing the foreman every day and going over the progress that had been made. If it differed in any way from the weekly schedule that Craig had left for her, or if there were any other problems, she phoned his secretary. She never asked for Craig now, but once she rang when his secretary was out and he answered the phone. Charlotte was so overcome at unexpectedly hearing his voice that she could hardly speak and they had a very short and stilted conversation. Once, too, he came down on a Saturday when the builders hit a major problem. Charlotte saw him arrive and immediately went up to the attic floor where she could look down at the courtyard from one of the gable windows, but not be seen from the ground. She watched him keenly whenever he was in sight, but made no attempt to go and talk to him. It would be no use, they both knew it was over. Just before he left, Craig took a couple of steps towards the door leading to her wing and her heart stopped, but then he hesitated, glanced at her windows, then stuck his hands in his pockets and turned to walk quickly away.

They said that everyone forgot in time, but Charlotte didn't find it so. The wound didn't heal and there wasn't a day, or even an hour that went by that she didn't think of Craig. The builders had torn out all the rotten timbers and replaced them, and started on the actual alterations, but it was still as noisy and dirty. The weeks of summer gradually dwindled into autumn and the work went quickly on, but Charlotte began to wish it would go far more slowly, for when the work was finished there wouldn't even be Craig's weekly letter to look forward to.

During this time she turned down all offers of dates, but she did go out with Mike Brooks and his friends from the rugby club together with their girlfriends. In September the new season started and she was persuaded to watch a few matches and go to a dance being held to raise funds for the first team's forthcoming overseas tour. It was impossible not to enjoy the dance; three of the biggest, beefiest rugby players dressed up in forties-style women's dresses and wigs and did a hilarious take-off of the Andrews Sisters. And that was just the opening act of the cabaret! It was the early hours of the morning before it was over and Mike was in no state to drive, but Charlotte had come in his car and had no other way to get home.

'I'll drive,' she told him. 'Open all the windows and maybe it will help you sober up.'

But when they reached the Abbey she saw that he was still too tipsy to drive, so she helped him inside and made him some black coffee. Mike drank it, but then yawned mightily and fell asleep on the sofa! Even vigorous shaking wouldn't waken him, so Charlotte took pity on him and found a blanket and pillow before going into the next room to collapse into her own bed.

The next day was Saturday, and the builders always worked on Saturday mornings. They had got past the stage of wolf-whistles and facetious remarks and had some respect for her by now, but there was no way Charlotte wanted to give them food for gossip and more innuendoes for months to come by letting them find that a man had stayed the night. So she set her alarm for seven and when it went off dragged herself out of bed and put on a robe and slippers to go wake Mike.

She shook him, shouted, and in the end let her alarm clock go off an inch away from his ear before he finally awoke.

'What is it? What's the matter?' he asked, his voice still slurred.

'You've got to go home. No, don't go back to sleep. Get up and wash.'

Sitting up, Mike gave a groan and put a hand to his head, then looked owlishly around him. 'What am I doing here? This is your place.'

'Yes, you passed out last night. Come on, I'll show you where the bathroom is and you can have a wash while I make you some coffee.'

'What's the time?' He managed to get his watch-face in focus and gave a howl of indignation. 'It's only seven o'clock!'

He started to lie back again, but Charlotte grabbed him. 'No, don't go back to sleep. The builders start at eight; you must be gone by then.'

'Oh, Charlie, for heaven's sake! Who cares? We haven't done anything.'

'They don't know that. And I've got to live with them for months yet. You haven't. So will you please pull yourself together and go?'

Eventually she managed to get him into the bathroom and had a very strong coffee waiting for him when he came out ten minutes later, looking unshaven and the worse for wear, but at least reasonably with-it. Over coffee they talked and laughed about the dance, but at seven-thirty Charlotte looked pointedly at her watch and Mike stood up with a groan. 'God, my head aches! You'd think I'd learn, but every rugby club dance is the same.'

The morning was cool as Charlotte opened the door for him, and she shivered, pulling her robe closer over her thin nightdress. Mike's car was parked right outside the door and he said, 'Go in, don't catch cold. See you, Charlie. Thanks for putting me up.'

Charlotte nodded and closed the door, deciding to go back to bed for a couple of hours. But she'd only been there for five minutes when someone banged on the main door. Cursing, she got out of bed again and went to open it. It was Mike. 'The car won't start,' he informed her. 'Can I use your phone?'

'But it must start, it was perfectly all right last night.'

'Well, it won't now. The battery's dead.'

'But how? I...' A thought occurred to her. 'Oh no, I didn't leave the lights on, did I?'

Mike grinned. ''Fraid so.' And he started to step back in.

'Oh, no, you don't. You can take my car,' she told him, pushing him out on to the step, her arm round his waist.

But before Charlotte had time to go back for her keys, another car drove through the gatehouse arch and into the courtyard. Damn! The builders were early. But the car was a dark blue Porsche, and it was Craig who flung open the door and got quickly out at the sight of them.

He strode towards them, his face a thundercloud, and Charlotte suddenly realised how it must look to him, her in her robe and nightdress, her hair dishevelled and her arm round Mike's waist. And Mike, unshaven and in an evening suit, so obviously having spent the night there. She gave an agonised look at Craig's face and ran back into the house, abandoning poor Mike while she frantically searched for her keys. Behind her, she heard the men speaking, Craig's voice cold and belligerent. But at least they hadn't come to blows. Finding the keys in her bedside drawer, Charlotte ran back and thrust them into

Mike's hand. 'Here you are. You can pick up your car some other time.'

'OK.' But he gave Craig a frowning look.

Charlotte went to go inside, but Craig said sharply, 'I'd like to speak to you.'

'Won't it do later? I have to...'

'No, now!' he snapped, his jaw thrust forward.

'If you'd like me to stay, Charlie...' Mike began.

But she took another look at Craig's icy face and said, 'Oh, no, that's all right, thanks, Mike. Craig only wants to talk about the builders' work. He's the architect, you know.'

So Mike left, if somewhat dubiously, and Craig followed Charlotte inside. By now she was shivering, but not only from cold. He looked so furiously angry. As she turned to face him, Charlotte's heart quailed for a moment. 'I take it it *is* the house you want to talk about?'

'No, it damn well isn't,' Craig answered hotly. 'What the hell was he doing here? Or shouldn't I ask?' he added scornfully.

'No, you shouldn't.'

He stared at her, his lips drawn back into a snarl.

'You don't waste any time, do you?'

Embarrassed at being found in such a ridiculous situation, and angry that Craig had jumped to the wrong conclusion without even giving her the opportunity of an explanation, Charlotte bristled with indignation. 'And what's that supposed to mean?'

'It means that it sure as hell didn't take you long to get over me, did it? Less than a month ago you were ready to go to bed with me—and you're already going with someone else!'

'Shut up! It isn't like that. I haven't...'

But Craig was too angry to listen. Catching her wrist, he pulled her towards him and glared down at her. 'You used to go out with him before we met. Did you go to bed with him then, too—or is it only since you split with me?'

'Stop it! I don't have to listen to this!'

She tried to break free, but Craig pulled her roughly back. There was utter fury in his eyes, the face of a man who had been pushed too far and was on the point of losing control of emotions too long held in check.

'My God, to think that I was worried about you being alone here! No wonder you didn't move out or have a friend stay. All the time you were going to bed with someone else behind my back!'

'No! No, Craig, it isn't like that. I didn't go to bed with him. And I've only seen him a few times since we broke up...'

'Well, at least you have the decency to go with only one man at a time,' he sneered in derisive fury.

'No, that isn't what I meant. I haven't...'

But Craig was so angry that he ignored her protests and swept on, 'It seems that you're not so different from Verity, after all. Off with one man and on with the new.'

'Leave Verity out of this!'

The sharp fierceness of her tone ripped through Craig's rage, but only gave him another reason to fuel it. 'I was as patient with you as I knew how; worrying about your jealousy over Verity, trying to convince you that there was nothing between us. I thought that over-fertile imagination of yours was always painting pictures of me with Verity and it was that you couldn't take. That there was a psychological barrier you just couldn't overcome. But maybe that wasn't it at all. Maybe you wanted to play the same kind of game Verity does: keeping your options open, having as many men on your string as possible. I...'

Raising her free hand, Charlotte hit him across the face. It wasn't a hard blow, and anyway Craig saw it coming and jerked his head back, but even so the sound of the slap had the effect of a pistol shot, and abruptly cut off his tirade of rage. For a moment he stared at her white, angry face in almost stunned disbelief, and it was obvious that no woman had ever slapped him before.

'Why, you little...' He lunged at Charlotte, grabbing hold of her and bending her backwards as he took her mouth in a kiss of furious passion. He was so angry that he didn't care whether she responded or not, he only wanted to dominate and possess. To vent his anger by subjecting her to his will, to master her by the force of his overpowering strength and fury.

For a few moments Charlotte struggled wildly, beating ineffectually at his shoulders with her fists. But it only made him tighten his arms and pin her hard against him, and his mouth ravage hers all the more. She made angry sounds of protest and struggled again, but now her body was held close to Craig's, and when she moved against him it triggered off a great surge of yearning deep down inside her. She moaned, wanting him, wanting love. Her hands gripped his shoulders and she deliberately pressed her hips against his, her mouth opening under the on-slaught of his kiss.

Craig was still so full of rage, so overpowered by it, that it was some moments before he realised what she was doing. When he did, a great tremor ran through him and he groaned, deep in his throat. He ground out her name, over and over, and began to kiss her neck, her throat, his lips avid and his breathing ragged. His hand went to the neck of her nightgown and thrust the material impatiently aside, his lips scorching her skin as he went on down.

'Oh, Craig!' She kissed him greedily, her hands in his hair, too hungry, too impatient for his touch to wait. She wanted him so much, her body on fire with a need that only he could fulfil. A lifetime without love was too long, too long. 'Oh, Craig. Oh, my love!' She panted out the words against his mouth, revelling in the passion that she had aroused in him.

Her robe was thrown aside and Craig's lips were on her breast, still passionately possessive, still hard and demanding, so that she cried out at the almost unbearable sensuousness of it. His hands were on her skin, bruising her flesh as he caressed and explored her, making her gasp and her moans mingle with his. She began to pull at his shirt, but there were too many buttons.

Stooping, he picked her up in his arms and carried her through to the bedroom. Charlotte put her arms round his neck and kissed him fiercely as he did so, so that he bumped against the wall and the doorway. When they reached it he set her down and put his hand in her hair, the other one on her hips, holding her against him as he kissed her with all the frustrated yearning of the weeks that they'd been apart.

'Oh, Craig, my darling,' she groaned as he kissed her throat. 'I missed you so!'

He raised his head to stare at her, his body trembling in feverish desire, his breath a shuddering moan of hunger, his face taut with passion and his eyes dark with anticipation. They dwelt on her face for a long moment, seeing hunger and excitement there, then slid past her to the bed. He went to pick her up, to carry her to it— but then he stopped and slowly straightened.

Charlotte felt his body stiffen, grow rigid, and she raised puzzled eyes to his face. He had gone very white and his breathing was still uneven, but with sudden anger again. Abruptly he let her go and took an unsteady step away from her.

'Craig? What is it?' She swung round to look behind her, saw the crumpled bed and suddenly understood. 'Craig, it isn't what you think. I didn't sleep with him, honestly. He...'

But he gave a strangled cry and strode out of the room, pushing her out of the way as he did so.

'Craig, wait!' She ran after him and caught his arm, making him stop and face her. 'You've got to listen to me! I didn't go to bed with Mike. He had too much to drink and...'

But he was far too angry to listen, only now his anger was the cold, controlled fury of a man who was doubly hurt. 'You witch!' he spat at her. 'And I thought Verity was a sex-cat! Compared with you she's an innocent!'

Charlotte's face went deathly pale as she stared at him. 'Craig, you're wrong.'

'I certainly am,' he agreed bitingly before she could go on. 'My God, was I wrong—about you. Tell me, did it turn you on to lure me into your bed while it was still hot from your last man?' A look of scornful disgust came into his eyes.

He tried to shake her off and make for the door, but Charlotte barred his way, her own anger rising. 'How *dare* you speak to me like that? And you know it isn't true. You *know* I'm not like that.'

'No? And just how am I supposed to know it?'

'Because your own instincts tell you so. Only you're so damn jealous that you won't listen to them.'

Craig laughed harshly. 'Me? Jealous? That's funny! That's really funny, coming from you. And now that it's the other way round, I'm supposed to know instinctively that what I see in front of my eyes isn't true. Isn't that what you're saying?' He was still fumingly angry, his hands bunched into tight fists as he shot the scornful words at her.

'It isn't the way it looks,' Charlotte insisted, and then, helplessly, in the face of his anger, 'Yes, that's what I'm saying; you ought to know me well enough...'

'But you knew me just as well,' Craig cut in forcefully, 'yet you never believed a word I said. It was always Verity you believed, Verity's poison that you let come between us. You said that you loved me—but you had no instinctive trust in me. So why the hell should I have any in you?'

Charlotte stared at him, only faintly beginning to realise the torment he had gone through. She reached out to put a hand on his arm, opened her mouth to speak. But her words were drowned by a loud concert of motor horns and cat calls right outside the window. The builders had arrived. 'Wakey, wakey!' they shouted in raucous humour. 'Time to start work!'

Craig swore and, shaking off her hand, strode out to the courtyard. He was greeted by shouts of laughter and a whole lot of remarks that made Charlotte go red as she listened by the window. The builders, seeing Craig's Porsche there, had obviously jumped to the conclusion that *he* had spent the night with her. Charlotte sat down on the bed, very close to tears. There were some days when you just couldn't win!

But what had happened that morning made her think long and hard. To get some peace and quiet she went out across the hills, the fields heavy with ripening wheat. But her mind was introspective, going back over her relationship with Craig and trying to see things through his eyes. She realised that all along she had taken Verity's word against his, even though she knew that her sister got a kick out of taking men from other women. But Verity had been taking things from her for so long, and Charlotte had such a deep-rooted fear of her powers, that she'd shrunk from any contest and been ready to believe anything Verity said. And because of that she'd let Verity win, in this, the most important thing in her life.

But perhaps not quite. Craig's loss of control today had made Charlotte see just how badly she'd hurt him, and how deep his emotions went. And the fact that she hadn't been able to convince him of her innocence had been an eye-opener too. It had been like trying to break through a solid wall of disbelief and prejudice. Not a nice experience, and one that Craig had been going through for weeks because of her phobia about Verity. But Verity, thank God, had gone back to America to marry her film director, satisfied that she had got her own back on them both, and caring little about the wreckage she'd made of their lives.

But perhaps it wasn't too late. Again the thought came into Charlotte's mind, small and tentative, a hope that she was almost afraid to nurture. But, if Craig could get that jealous, didn't that mean that there might still be a chance? If the way she'd failed to trust him hadn't made him too angry to care any more. If he would ever believe the truth about Mike. Charlotte went on gazing into space, but then came to a decision and went racing back to the house.

The telephone was a wonderful invention, and for Charlotte that day it worked miracles. It took time and lots of calls, but that evening she was able to lock up the Abbey, put a suitcase in the car and drive away with that small hope grown much larger in her heart.

The mist of early morning still lay on the ground next day when the first strings of horses were taken from their stables up to the Berkshire Downs.

Charlotte stood by the car near the track leading up to the hills, a pair of binoculars in her hands trained on the riders. She swept them along, searching for a familiar figure, stiffened and then relaxed in relief as Craig came into view. It was too far away to do anything but recognise him, and when he rode back towards the stables he was hidden among the string of riders, so she had no indication of his mood, could only hope that he wasn't still so furious that he would ignore her. The string turned into the track and the first of the riders began to pass her. Charlotte tossed the binoculars into the back of the car and walked forward to where she could easily be seen.

The horse he was riding started nervously back, surprised by the sudden jerk on the reins, but Craig recovered quickly and brought the horse back into line. His eyes were on her face, his own a mask that had come swiftly down over surprised vulnerability. The horse came on, and for a dreadful moment Charlotte thought he was going to ignore her. She half lifted her hand, but then Craig reined in and said harshly, 'What do you want?'

'To talk to you. Please.'

He hesitated, his face tightening, then dismounted and gave the reins to another rider, had a brief word with him, and then took off his hat and waited till all the string had gone by before he walked slowly over to her. He was wearing riding breeches and a thick sweater, his hair dishevelled and a glow of colour in his cheeks from the sharp breeze. He came and stood a little way from her, but didn't say anything, leaving her to make all the moves.

'I—I thought I'd find you here,' she ventured.

'So?' The word was snapped out at her.

Charlotte had come there prepared to be humble, to apologise abjectly, and beg and plead if that was what it was going to take, but his tone made her chin come up. 'I came here,' she said shortly, 'to tell you I love you. I know I've been a fool and I'm sorry. I know I should have trusted you, but I didn't. But you know the reasons and I'm not going to make any excuses. It—it happened.' She paused, chest heaving as she sought for words, finding this a hell of a lot harder than she'd ever imagined.

'So?' Craig said again derisively.

'Oh, for heaven's sake stop saying "So?" like a choirboy who's stuck on one note! So I'm telling you that I've come to you. If you want me. So I'm trusting you—with myself. And I'm asking you to trust me in return. If you can.' She twisted her hands together and brought them up to her face in an involuntary gesture of pleading, biting her knuckles as she waited.

Craig looked at her, his face hard and unreadable, and was silent for so long that she turned away in despair and began to walk stumblingly back to the car.

'Wait!'

His voice brought her up short and she swung round with hope surging through her heart. But his face was still hard and unrelenting.

'What do you mean—you're trusting me with yourself?'

Trying to speak calmly, Charlotte said, 'I've left the Abbey. I've taken the mare back and given my pony away. I've resigned from my job. I've put my whole past behind me so that we can start from new, from this moment. I have nothing in the world now but you.'

His eyes had widened as Craig listened to her, his face losing its tension as he stared at her in growing wonder. 'That's—that's some commitment,' he said unsteadily.

'I wanted it to be. I wanted you to know that nothing else matters to me but you. I wanted you to be absolutely sure of that. And I want you to believe that there was nothing between Mike and me on Friday night. He got drunk and stayed the night on the sofa—and that was all.'

She looked at him pleadingly, unable to keep the fear of rejection out of her voice. Craig gazed at her for a long moment and then sighed. 'We'd better go back to my place and talk this out.'

Relief flooded through her veins and she smiled at him weakly. 'I have a better idea. Why don't we go back to my place?'

He looked at her sharply. 'Your place? But I thought you'd left the Abbey?'

'I have.' She took a key-ring from her pocket and held it up. 'You know you said you'd always wanted a cottage here—well, I rented one. It's pretty small, only one bedroom. But the bed is king-size and . . .'

But Craig's face had broken into a huge grin and he came and put his arms round her waist. 'How far is it?'

'Two minutes in the car.'

'Then what are we waiting for?' He smiled down at her, his eyes already darkening, and when he kissed her his lips were possessive again.

Charlotte slipped her arms round his neck and looked searchingly into his face. 'You believe me—about Mike?'

'Mm.' He lifted his head. 'I think I always did. It was just that jealousy took over from basic instincts for a while.'

She gave a rueful laugh. 'I know the feeling!' She looked up at him, her eyes suddenly drowned in tears, and Craig kissed her fiercely, his arms tight around her, letting her know that everything was all right.

When he at last released her, Charlotte smiled at him mistily as he put his arm round her waist and began to walk her to the car. But as they reached it she stopped and said, 'Craig? When we reach the cottage . . .'

'Yes?' He turned to look at her.

'Do we—do we have to *talk*?'

He laughed, a rich, masculine laugh of happiness that was good to hear. 'Of course we have to talk.' He waited until her mouth dropped a little before adding, 'But much—much later. First there's a lot of other catching up we have to do.' His eyes held her. 'My love. My *only* love,' he stressed.

And Charlotte knew then that this man was hers, and only hers, for the rest of their lives together.

Coming Next Month

1223 DEEP HARBOUR Sally Cook
Lucy had enjoyed the summer with her aunt's family in Minorca until strange things started to happen. Unafraid, she decides to investigate, only to discover that everything seems to lead back to a mysterious man in one of the villas.

1224 ONE HOUR OF MAGIC Melinda Cross
Robert Chesterfield had been full of light and laughter, while Daniel, his brother, had been so dark and brooding. Now, with Robert dead and Daniel providing her with a home and a job, Holly wonders how she can live with someone who hated the man she loved.

1225 LOVEKNOT Catherine George
Sophie's life had always been planned by those around her, particularly her father and brothers. Now everything is changing, and Sophie plans to change, too. Then why is it so difficult to leave her aloof, unapproachable boss, nicknamed Alexander the Great?

1226 REMEMBER TOMORROW Pamela Hatton
Powerful, arrogant Ross Tyler is fighting painful injuries as well as the belief that Cassie had deserted him after the car crash. When they finally chance to meet, Ross discovers that Cassie didn't even know he was alive.

1227 THE LOVING GIFT Carole Mortimer
David Kendrick falls in love with Jade at first sight—but that doesn't mean she has to put up with his impulsive pursuit. He might be charming, but since she's still running away from a hurtful past, surely it's better not to start anything?

1228 DON'T ASK WHY Annabel Murray
Why is the stranger in the astrakhan coat following her husband? Determined to find out, Giana's search soon leads her to greater confusion and a life of lies and subterfuge in the employ of the semireclusive Breid Winterton.

1229 MAN WITHOUT A PAST Valerie Parv
"Don't love me, Gaelle," Dan warns her, "for your own sake." But it is already far too late to tell her that. And neither of them can foresee just how impossible their love is.

1230 UNWILLING HEART Emma Richmond
O'Malley coped with being buried alive in an earthquake in Turkey—and having to dig her way out. But being kidnapped by a mysterious Frenchman, whom she knows only as Paget, is another matter entirely!

Available in December wherever paperback books are sold, or through Harlequin Reader Service:

In the U.S.
901 Fuhrmann Blvd.
P.O. Box 1397
Buffalo, N.Y. 14240-1397

In Canada
P.O. Box 603
Fort Erie, Ontario
L2A 5X3

Have You Ever Wondered If You Could Write A Harlequin Novel?

Here's great news—Harlequin is offering a series of cassette tapes to help you do just that. Written by Harlequin editors, these tapes give practical advice on how to make your characters—and your story—come alive. There's a tape for each contemporary romance series Harlequin publishes.

Mail order only

All sales final

TO: **Harlequin Reader Service**
Audiocassette Tape Offer
P.O. Box 1396
Buffalo, NY   14269-1396

I enclose a check/money order payable to HARLEQUIN READER SERVICE® for $9.70 ($8.95 plus 75¢ postage and handling) for EACH tape ordered for the total sum of $_____*
Please send:

☐ Romance and Presents   ☐ Intrigue
☐ American Romance   ☐ Temptation
☐ Superromance   ☐ All five tapes ($38.80 total)

Signature_____
                                              (please print clearly)
Name:_____
Address:_____
State:_____ Zip:_____

*Iowa and New York residents add appropriate sales tax.

AUDIO-H

INDULGE A LITTLE SWEEPSTAKES
OFFICIAL RULES
SWEEPSTAKES RULES AND REGULATIONS. NO PURCHASE NECESSARY.

1. NO PURCHASE NECESSARY. To enter complete the official entry form and return with the invoice in the envelope provided. Or you may enter by printing your name, complete address and your daytime phone number on a 3 x 5 piece of paper. Include with your entry the hand printed words "Indulge A Little Sweepstakes." Mail your entry to: Indulge A Little Sweepstakes, P.O. Box 1397, Buffalo, NY 14269-1397. No mechanically reproduced entries accepted. Not responsible for late, lost, misdirected mail, or printing errors.

2. Three winners, one per month (Sept. 30, 1989, October 31, 1989 and November 30, 1989), will be selected in random drawings. All entries received prior to the drawing date will be eligible for that month's prize. This sweepstakes is under the supervision of MARDEN-KANE, INC. an independent judging organization whose decisions are final and binding. Winners will be notified by telephone and may be required to execute an affidavit of eligibility and release which must be returned within 14 days, or an alternate winner will be selected.

3. Prizes: 1st Grand Prize (1) a trip for two to Disneyworld in Orlando, Florida. Trip includes round trip air transportation, hotel accommodations for seven days and six nights, plus up to $700 expense money (ARV $3,500). 2nd Grand Prize (1) a seven-night Chandris Caribbean Cruise for two includes transportation from nearest major airport, accommodations, meals plus up to $1,000 in expense money (ARV $4,300). 3rd Grand Prize (1) a ten-day Hawaiian holiday for two includes round trip air transportation for two, hotel accommodations, sightseeing, plus up to $1,200 in spending money (ARV $7,700). All trips subject to availability and must be taken as outlined on the entry form.

4. Sweepstakes open to residents of the U.S. and Canada 18 years or older except employees and the families of Torstar Corp., its affiliates, subsidiaries and Marden-Kane, Inc. and all other agencies and persons connected with conducting this sweepstakes. All Federal, State and local laws and regulations apply. Void wherever prohibited or restricted by law. Taxes, if any are the sole responsibility of the prize winners. Canadian winners will be required to answer a skill testing question. Winners consent to the use of their name, photograph and/or likeness for publicity purposes without additional compensation.

5. For a list of prize winners, send a stamped, self-addressed envelope to Indulge A Little Sweepstakes Winners, P.O. Box 701, Sayreville, NJ 08871.

© 1989 HARLEQUIN ENTERPRISES LTD.

DL-SWPS

INDULGE A LITTLE SWEEPSTAKES
OFFICIAL RULES
SWEEPSTAKES RULES AND REGULATIONS. NO PURCHASE NECESSARY.

1. NO PURCHASE NECESSARY. To enter complete the official entry form and return with the invoice in the envelope provided. Or you may enter by printing your name, complete address and your daytime phone number on a 3 x 5 piece of paper. Include with your entry the hand printed words "Indulge A Little Sweepstakes." Mail your entry to: Indulge A Little Sweepstakes, P.O. Box 1397, Buffalo, NY 14269-1397. No mechanically reproduced entries accepted. Not responsible for late, lost, misdirected mail, or printing errors.

2. Three winners, one per month (Sept. 30, 1989, October 31, 1989 and November 30, 1989), will be selected in random drawings. All entries received prior to the drawing date will be eligible for that month's prize. This sweepstakes is under the supervision of MARDEN-KANE, INC. an independent judging organization whose decisions are final and binding. Winners will be notified by telephone and may be required to execute an affidavit of eligibility and release which must be returned within 14 days, or an alternate winner will be selected.

3. Prizes: 1st Grand Prize (1) a trip for two to Disneyworld in Orlando, Florida. Trip includes round trip air transportation, hotel accommodations for seven days and six nights, plus up to $700 expense money (ARV $3,500). 2nd Grand Prize (1) a seven-night Chandris Caribbean Cruise for two includes transportation from nearest major airport, accommodations, meals plus up to $1,000 in expense money (ARV $4,300). 3rd Grand Prize (1) a ten-day Hawaiian holiday for two includes round trip air transportation for two, hotel accommodations, sightseeing, plus up to $1,200 in spending money (ARV $7,700). All trips subject to availability and must be taken as outlined on the entry form.

4. Sweepstakes open to residents of the U.S. and Canada 18 years or older except employees and the families of Torstar Corp., its affiliates, subsidiaries and Marden-Kane, Inc. and all other agencies and persons connected with conducting this sweepstakes. All Federal, State and local laws and regulations apply. Void wherever prohibited or restricted by law. Taxes, if any are the sole responsibility of the prize winners. Canadian winners will be required to answer a skill testing question. Winners consent to the use of their name, photograph and/or likeness for publicity purposes without additional compensation.

5. For a list of prize winners, send a stamped, self-addressed envelope to Indulge A Little Sweepstakes Winners, P.O. Box 701, Sayreville, NJ 08871.

© 1989 HARLEQUIN ENTERPRISES LTD.

DL-SWPS

INDULGE A LITTLE—WIN A LOT!

Summer of '89 Subscribers-Only Sweepstakes

OFFICIAL ENTRY FORM

This entry must be received by: October 31, 1989
This month's winner will be notified by: Nov. 7, 1989
Trip must be taken between: Dec. 7, 1989–April 7, 1990
(depending on sailing schedule)

YES, I want to win the Caribbean cruise vacation for two! I understand the prize includes round-trip airfare, a one-week cruise including private cabin and all meals, and a daily allowance as revealed on the "Wallet" scratch-off card.

Name_____

Address_____

City_____State/Prov._____Zip/Postal Code_____

Daytime phone number_____
Area code

Return entries with invoice in envelope provided. Each book in this shipment has two entry coupons — and the more coupons you enter, the better your chances of winning!

© 1989 HARLEQUIN ENTERPRISES LTD.

DINDL-2